He sensed that she was trying to get him involved, throw him off guard. He saw the danger, and resisted it. He *would* pursue her relentlessly, even drawing her into his romantic orbit.

But romance wasn't on his agenda.

Murder, the bottom line, had been penciled in...

The Word on William Katz's Previous Thrillers is...

"Gripping."   —*New York Times*

"Chilling."   —*United Press International*

"Taut."   —*Chicago Sun-Times*

"Exciting."   —*West Coast Review of Books*

"Sensational."   —*Publishers Weekly*

"Breathless."   —*New York Times*

Also by William Katz

Death Dreams
Open House
Surprise Party

Published by
WARNER BOOKS

WILLIAM KATZ

AFTER DARK

WARNER BOOKS

A Warner Communications Company

WARNER BOOKS EDITION

Cover illustration by Sonja and Nenad Jakesvic

Warner Books, Inc.
666 Fifth Avenue
New York, N.Y. 10103

A Warner Communications Company

Printed in the United States of America

First Printing: July, 1988

10 9 8 7 6 5 4 3 2 1

Prologue

He knew him.

At least he knew the face. He'd seen so many faces go by him during his years in family court—embittered teenagers, scared yet defiant, meek yet capable of the most horrible crimes. Had he been one of them? He had to be. Why else would he be approaching so quickly, with that glint in his eye?

But what did he want?

What was he reaching for?

Why was he carrying that big plastic bag over his left arm?

Yes, he *was* one of them. He remembered him now. He was that kid who . . .

His thoughts were broken by the shattering crack of a bullet.

He only felt, in that final second, a blow to his head, as if someone had punched him.

And as he fell, he looked up and saw the grin that he'd

once pledged he'd never forget. The owner of that grin
never forgot either.

The world went black.

The grin became broader.

1

"I want to sleep."

Anne mumbled it to herself. There was no one to hear her. She'd been mumbling it every night for three months, knowing she wouldn't get her wish.

Chronic insomnia.

A curse, she'd told her doctor. A medical condition, he'd told her. May be physical. Probably psychiatric. They'd take tests. Many, many tests.

It was three o'clock on a balmy spring night. Anne's left eye opened automatically, precisely on schedule, and she instantly felt the burning of strained muscles and the ache of exhaustion. She also felt nauseated, the feeling someone gets when the body has been racked by sleeplessness for months. It wasn't fair. It was consuming her.

Her right eye opened. Fight it, she ordered herself. Fight it and maybe you can beat it. But she knew all her subliminal cheerleading would result in nothing. She'd been here too many times before.

At thirty-three, Anne Seibert feared she'd started looking old. She was a free-lance publicity writer in New York City, and she knew that the insomnia was starting to affect her writing. She was spelling words wrong, getting sentences confused, losing thoughts. The glib little phrases of her trade weren't flowing anymore. She'd overheard someone whisper that she was probably a drunk. That was killing her almost as much as the insomnia was.

Now, still lying in bed, only a wisp of moonlight flickering in through a window, she started her nightly routine of trying to get back to sleep. She took a deep, audible breath, then tried to relax. She thought of waves washing up on shore and imagined hearing the soothing sound that accompanied them. And she counted sheep—about four hundred every night.

But she wouldn't take pills. Addictive, the doctor said. So she suffered.

New Rochelle, N.Y.

Mark Chaney saw the New Rochelle exit and lurched over to the right lane of the Hutchinson River Parkway, the "Hutch" to any seasoned New Yorker. As his Jaguar swerved, he heard that familiar thump in the trunk. It always rolled around, he thought to himself. Maybe some blankets back there would help, or some old tires from the basement. He didn't want it bruised. If it was bruised he'd have to patch it up. He had to stop that rolling around. It bothered him. Especially at 3:00 A.M., when there weren't too many other road noises.

He pulled off the Hutch at the New Rochelle exit and drove immediately to a deserted service station. He'd often pulled in here late at night because it had a public phone that invariably worked. He inched the Jaguar around to the back of the station, where it couldn't be seen from the road, yanked on some gloves to make fingerprints impossible, and slipped into the phone booth. He dialed a number. The phone at the other end rang.

Someone picked it up.

"Hello? Mark, is it you?"

"Yes, Emil, it's me."

"All taken care of?"

"It's taken care of," Chaney replied. "It's all finished."

"This meant a lot to me," Emil said. "I think you know how much it meant."

"To both of us. You feel better, Emil?"

"Sure. I'm getting up and having some Frusen Gladje chocolate."

"Then you feel good."

"I wish we could have a party right now," Emil said. "We've waited for this for years. Look, maybe we'll throw a party for ourselves in a couple of weeks."

"Why not?" Chaney answered. "We deserve it. We've done this perfectly. When you do things perfectly, you deserve to celebrate."

They spoke a few minutes longer, then each hung up. Chaney left the booth and slid back into the brown leather seat of his Jaguar. He loved that squeak of the leather, the sweet sound of financial success that those people never thought he'd achieve, success that he could savor even on a night like this. He started the engine and pulled out of the station, again hearing the thump behind him. Blankets next time, he thought.

Mark Chaney was thirty-six, tall and rugged-looking, impeccably dressed in a custom Dunhill suit, his gold and steel Rolex submariner glistening on his wrist. He was a

ladies' man, with a charm and smoothness ripped
from a magazine ad. In fact, he'd once been featured
as "most eligible bachelor" in a major women's magazine.

But, to any policeman cruising by he was also the
successful suburban businessman coming home late from
meetings. He'd nurtured that image for years, often holding
all-night sessions with associates just to establish his credibility as someone willing to work twenty-four hours if
business demanded it.

He started into one of the better residential sections of
New Rochelle, gliding past the colonials and split-levels,
some with eager "for sale" signs outside.

The thumping in the trunk stopped now, calmed by
smooth roads and slow speeds. Above the hum of the motor
Chaney could hear only the crackling of some trees in the
spring breeze.

He wondered, as he approached his neighborhood, whether
he would see it again—that light in the house across the
street. He'd seen it three or four times now, and it was
beginning to bother him, like the thumping in the trunk.
He'd met the young woman who lived in that house—
Anne Seibert—only a few times. He'd helped her get her
lemonlike Oldsmobile started once. She'd moved in only
three months earlier, and the light started coming on at
3:00 A.M. about six weeks after she arrived. He knew—
because the neighborhood grapevine told him—that she
was a publicity writer in the city, that she'd just gone
through a wrenching divorce, that her former husband
apparently was violent, and that she rented the house.
That's all he knew . . . except that she turned that light on
every night.

Why did she turn it on?

What did she find so interesting at that hour?

Why did she move across the street from him?

He was a worrier, Mark Chaney told himself. Always the worrier. But why not? He had plenty to worry about. Enemies were all over. They always had been. Watching him. Waiting to hurt him.

The night scared Anne.

It was the sounds.

Sounds that were ignored by day were terrors by night, conjuring up frightful images and wild exaggerations. A snapping twig was woodsy by day. At night it was a prowler. A car engine at 3:00 P.M. was a mother bringing her child from school. At 3:00 A.M. it was someone stalking the neighborhood. The sound of a voice at noon was a child laughing or a neighbor yakking. In pitch darkness it was someone sick, or scared, or being beaten. And a barking cocker spaniel? In the middle of the night it was a wolf pack.

The insomniac lives in a fearful world, a world of blackness, in which silence is normal, and any deviation a shock. To Anne, after dark was a dangerous time, a time of nightmares.

Her last two years had been so filled with real nightmares. Who could have guessed that the man she'd known since she was fifteen, whom she'd put through medical school, would become a walking bomb, threatening her every day, once almost hitting her with a bottle? Now he was "under therapy"—the polite name for it—but Anne always feared that he'd return some night, livid, crazed, and she was sure these bouts of insomnia had something to do with that fear.

Now she swung out of bed, as per her nightly ritual, and tossed back her long, light brown hair. She threw on her blue housecoat, one of the first gifts her husband had given her in their seven-year marriage, and started for the living room. She knew this insomnia attack would last at least two hours. At the end of it she'd be drained and exhausted, even before the day had begun. Already she was fighting the eyestrain that caused the front of her head to go tight, and sometimes to erupt in pain. She was going through the insomniac's real nightmare.

She flipped on the living room light and sat down with a copy of *Newsweek*.

She had to read.

Naturally, she turned to a feature on marriage. It only reminded her how lonely she really was, how alone in the middle of the night. She was ready for someone new, someone who would bring romance and warmth back into her life, someone who would take the place of the monster who'd once been beside her.

That would cure this curse of sleeplessness.

In the distance, she heard a car engine. She squeezed down farther on her soft couch.

Fear.

Mark Chaney turned into his block and drove down slowly, hoping the sound of the engine wouldn't wake the neighbors. He drifted to his house, a three-bedroom split-level on a quarter acre, with a garage oddly placed in the back. He took his foot off the accelerator, letting the car coast toward the driveway.

Then he saw it.

She had her light on again. And there was her silhouette, in the living room. She was reading or, probably, pretending to read.

And . . . yes, again she got up and peeked through the blind. Was it an act? Was she just curious about the sound of the car? All right, people could be curious about that at three in the morning. But this happened night after night.

He only glanced toward her window, then turned back, not wanting her to realize she'd been noticed. Why let on? Why put her on her guard?

Chaney turned into his gravel driveway, worried. She was watching him. Well, maybe not. Maybe it was all a coincidence. But this many times? She couldn't know about him, about these evening rides. No one knew. Then why was she watching him? What did she, or the people she worked for, know? Had something interfered with his and Emil's perfect plan?

He slipped the car behind the house, where it was shielded from the neighbors' eyes by huge shrubs and trees. Still, despite the protection, Chaney pulled the car into his garage. He got out, closing the car door as quietly as he could, and immediately rushed into the house through the back entrance.

Discreetly, he knelt down and peeked under a shade at the house across the street. Yes, she was still there, still looking through her blinds.

He hated her. Even though he'd met her only a few times, he began to loathe her. Why couldn't she leave him alone?

"I wonder where he goes," Anne wrote in the little, red leather-bound diary that she'd started keeping to stay busy during her insomnia bouts. "Coming in here so often at three in the morning. Is he involved with the government in some way? Does he have a girlfriend? He's very good-looking and seems to be a successful businessman. I'd love to know him better. Really *love* to. But why these late-night trips?"

She looked through the blind, not realizing that Mark Chaney was peeking back. He was in a darkened room and could not be seen. The darkness struck her as odd as well. A man comes into his house and yet turns on no lights. Maybe he came in through the rear door in his garage, behind the house. Maybe he had a bedroom right near that door. What did it really matter? But the comings and goings of this night traveler were fascinating, especially to an insomniac.

Anne returned to reading *Newsweek*. The fatigue melted all over her. It would be another hellish day, trying to work, trying to keep her eyes open. Sometimes she almost wished she were dead.

Chaney returned to his car and opened the trunk. He stared down at the filled, green plastic bag that lay utterly still, shoved against the barrier that separated the trunk from the rear seat. The bag had bumped against a small carton that Chaney kept in the trunk and knocked over a spare bottle of transmission fluid. The neck of the bottle had leaked, staining the trunk carpet. Stupid, Chaney thought to himself. This couldn't be allowed to happen again. Jaguar charged a fortune to replace those rugs.

Chaney took a deep breath to summon his strength, then grabbed at the bag and yanked it toward him. He lifted it out of the trunk, making sure not to scrape it against the trunk lock, and heaved it over his shoulder. He felt the gradually increasing stiffness of the contents, and it gave him a genuine thrill. This was accomplishment. This was what the word *satisfaction* was all about.

Stooped slightly from the 165-pound weight, Chaney stumbled, regained his footing, and started trudging toward the rear entrance. He carried the package into the house and lowered it to the floor near the basement door. The door was double-combination locked, a rare precaution for an inside door leading only to a basement. Meticulously, Chaney operated the combination dial on each lock, opening both.

Then, he flipped on the basement light. No one would notice because all his basement windows were covered from the inside with wood paneling. From the outside it simply looked as if the basement had been finished.

He lifted the plastic bag again and carried it slowly downstairs, balancing himself carefully so as not to fall. He placed the bag beside a huge freezer. He opened the top. There was another, identical bag inside, also filled "Hi there," Chaney said, and flashed a nervous, twitching little smile.

He took the new bag and placed it inside the freezer. "Sweet dreams," he said, then closed the top.

He started toward the stairs but decided on a slight diversion, walking toward a door leading to a finished room. This door too was double-combination locked, and again he carefully opened each lock.

He opened the door. The room was dark, except for the small light that he now allowed in. He could barely make out the hospital-style bed, the straitjacket lying on a nearby chair. He could see the outlines of the judge's bench and the gavel resting atop it. "Have a rotten night," he whispered, closed the door, and locked it again.

He went upstairs, locked the main basement door and returned to his car, retrieving a Heckler and Koch 9-mm pistol. He saw that it needed some cleaning, so he took it into the house and placed it at the bottom of a kitchen drawer.

Then he went to his bedroom and flipped on the light.

There, Anne thought to herself, a light came on. But why this delay? It was bizarre, she thought. Absolutely bizarre.

A man comes into a house, stays in darkness for more than fifteen minutes, *then* turns on the light.

But she had more pressing things to think about. She tried to get back to bed, tried to sleep once more. This time she attempted to think about warm milk. She'd thought about warm milk during past insomnia attacks, and sometimes it seemed to help, maybe because warm milk itself, according to some authorities, helps the sleep process. Sleep, she told herself over and over.

But she couldn't. The insomnia overwhelmed her. She tossed and fretted, utterly frustrated by her inability to sleep. Her eyes, burning and raw, kept popping open, feeling three times their size.

Chaney prepared to drop into bed. But, before he did, he took one look out the front window.

She was there again.

It infuriated him.

She was peeking through that living-room window.

Actually, what Chaney saw was a small kink in the venetian blind, left there when Anne had stared out earlier. She wasn't even in the living room.

He pulled back from his window, not wanting to look as if he were snooping. But this woman was becoming an obsession, something he didn't need when he already had a perfectly suitable obsession.

What could he do about her? He certainly couldn't go to the police and claim she was a Peeping Tom. He couldn't threaten her. He couldn't send her angry letters that would make her even *more* suspicious.

But maybe, he thought, he could trip her up in some way. Maybe, by doing the unexpected, he could make her reveal just what she was after, why she kept staring at his house night after night. Chaney eyed his phone. It was logical, he thought. One neighbor to another. Old-fashioned human concern. It was a noble thing, and no one could object.

He didn't know Anne's number, but knew her last name. He reached for the thin local directory near his phone and started looking up her name, his index finger racing down the page with the Se's. He went past her once, then went back, found the number, and dialed.

Anne jumped as the phone rang.

It had to be a wrong number—either that or some emergency. Maybe someone was sick. Maybe someone had been killed.

Still in bed, she reached over and grasped the receiver.

But wait. Maybe it's an obscene call, she thought. Don't answer it.

No, she had to answer it. Someone *could* be sick.

She lifted the receiver. "Hello?"

"Anne?"

She hesitated. She wasn't sure of that voice. "Yes."

"This is your neighbor, Mark Chaney, from across the street."

It was *him*. Incredible, but it was *him*. He sounded so charming, so warm, so much the mellow voice she would want to hear at this hour of the night. But why was he calling? Did he detect her? Was he angry? Anne was experiencing instant mortification of the adolescent variety.

"Hi," she replied, clearly startled by a call at this hour.

"I was up and saw your light, Anne. Is anything wrong?"

"Oh, no," Anne replied. "I was just doing some work."

"At this hour?"

"Sometimes I have to." She hated to admit she had insomnia. People still associated it with depression, or even drugs. "I have these deadlines," she said. "I know it's crazy."

"Well, I've got a lot of night work, too. I come in at all hours. But, look, I was just concerned. If anything ever is wrong, please call me. I mean that."

"Oh, . . . thank you. That's so nice."

What a great guy, she thought. OK, he came in at all hours, just as he said. But he was concerned, and he thought enough to call. Their conversation ended, and Anne rolled over in bed, a smile on her face for the first time in days. She hardly knew Mark Chaney, and yet he showed this interest. He liked her. It was obvious. She hadn't realized it before.

What a funny night—first insomnia, then wondering about that guy across the street, then that call. Maybe it was fate, Anne thought. Maybe fate had dictated that she wake up and attract Mark Chaney's attention. She suddenly liked that kind of fate. It made for great romances. It was the life-saving kind of fate.

Chaney slammed down his phone in disgust.

Did she really think he believed her? Who works at 4:00 A.M. when they have to get up early? She was a charmer, trying to put something over on him. He hated people like that. They'd always tried to fool him, to trick him, to get something from him.

She was lying . . . obviously.

She was watching him, and he was determined to find out why . . . and put an end to it.

He was an expert at putting an end to things.

2

Since Mark Chaney was co-owner of his own firm, he had the luxury of going in late after a night's work. He was in bed at 8:00 A.M. when Anne left her house and slammed her front door shut. The sound alerted Chaney, who moved to a window and discreetly looked out, wondering what Anne Seibert would look like after her late-night spying. He saw her walk slowly to her '82 Olds Omega, which was parked in the driveway. She had little of the bounce that most young women would have when first going to work. Even at this distance he saw that she was exhausted.

It was all so strange. *Could* she have been telling the truth after all? Had she been working late? All right, some people do work late occasionally, in a crisis, in an emergency, even if it means exhaustion the next day. But Anne seemed to be up in the middle of the night all the time, or all the times Chaney came in late. No, it wasn't right. It wasn't right at all.

As Anne pulled out of the driveway, Chaney went back to bed. He knew she would be on his agenda the second he got

into the office, for she could be dangerous, and Emil had to
be told.

It was another rotten morning for Anne. She drove her
rattletrap into Manhattan, trying to get the best radio sound
possible from an antenna that was stuck halfway up. She
feared the ride, the possibility of falling asleep at the wheel
and careening into some driver who'd exact retribution with
a baseball bat. So she turned the radio up higher than usual,
hoping the sound would keep her awake.

Ironic. Now she wanted to *stay* awake. Another cruel joke
that biology played on the insomniac.

She could have made her schedule more flexible and
gotten more sleep regularly, but that would have meant
giving up lucrative assignments. Together, they added up to
$28,000 a year, and she needed every cent of it.

Inevitably, despite the blare of the distorted speaker, she
thought of Mark Chaney. His house had been so still when
she'd left, and she figured that he wouldn't be going into work
until much later. What did he do that gave him this privi-
lege, yet required him to come in at all hours? She was
becoming fascinated by the guy, a fascination magnified by
his middle-of-the-night neighborliness and his very charm.
All right, she realized, she was plotting. Get to know him.
Figure out a way.

She was oblivious to a radio newsman reporting the
disappearance of a retired family court judge from his
secluded home in Scarsdale. She was too busy fighting
exhaustion and maneuvering through traffic. She didn't hear
the news that blood had been found just outside the judge's
home.

She paid her two dollars at the Triborough Bridge and
was almost clipped by another car when she pulled away

from the toll booth. The driver just looked back at her and made an obscene gesture. It was morning in New York.

Anne would be working today, and for the weeks ahead, at Stellar Motors, importers of the new FSR automobiles from West Germany, an assignment that made her rusting Olds even more of an embarrassment than it was ordinarily. She was under strict instructions to park it in a garage at least ten blocks from Stellar, and not to be seen inside it anywhere near the Stellar headquarters.

Anne followed the instructions, parked her remnant, and walked eleven blocks to Stellar's offices in a glass tower on Third Avenue in the forties. She bought a doughnut and a cup of coffee from a cart in the main hallway and rushed to her desk. One of her best friends worked at Stellar, and she couldn't wait to tell her about this new male find right in her own neighborhood, right across the street.

Mark Chaney got up at nine and immediately went to his basement to make sure the freezer was running properly. He looked in at his guests, still wrapped in green plastic bags, and knew that he and Emil would have their hands full the following weekend doing the necessary work. He hated when there were two. The work was hard enough with only one.

He got dressed and ready to leave, still intensely curious about Anne Seibert and why she was watching him. And so he decided to snoop around, to find out anything he could while Anne was away.

Chaney took a sugar bowl and left his house, walking slowly across the street to Anne's. Anyone watching him would have thought he was simply out to borrow some sugar, hardly a suspicious act. He walked up Anne's steps and rang the doorbell. Of course, there was no answer. But the feigned waiting gave him the chance to look in some of the windows. Maybe Anne had left something, in the security of her home, that would hint at why she'd become a late-night snoop.

The house looked innocuous enough, though. Chaney could see only into the living room and a guest room, but there was nothing out of the ordinary. There was a crumpled copy of *Newsweek* in the living room, along with some other magazines and a book. The guest room looked as if it had never been used.

Having rung the doorbell four or five times—enough for anyone watching him from another house to realize that he was getting no answer—he meandered around to the back door. There was a bell there too, and he rang it.

Again, he had a chance to look in some windows. And again, the scene was conventional. He'd learn nothing this way, he was sure.

And then, something caught his eye. It was resting on a table in the kitchen, almost hidden by a cookbook. It scared him, made him even more concerned that this woman was no innocent neighbor with a penchant for working late. What was she doing with that 35-mm Nikon camera with a telephoto lens? He'd never seen her with it outside the house. No one in the neighborhood had mentioned that she was interested in photography, and people with equipment like that usually were *very* interested. And, in his spying through her windows, he hadn't seen any photographs on display. Wouldn't someone interested in photography put pictures on display?

Was she snapping pictures of him? Were those pictures going to the police?

He knew he could be imagining things. He also knew he might *not* be imagining things. He'd find out. He had ways of finding out.

Chaney returned to his house and prepared to leave. He

snapped open his attaché case and placed inside it a manila folder that he'd kept in his bedroom. Inside the folder was information on a high school principal in Philadelphia: photographs of his house, his daily schedule, a map of his neighborhood, his complete family history. The information was important, for it would be the basis of the business meeting in three hours with Emil Welder.

Chaney locked the case, then brought it to the Jaguar and placed it in the spare-tire bin under the trunk. This was one thing that Chaney liked to keep hidden, the one thing he wouldn't want stolen from his car.

"So I'm sitting there in my living room reading this depressing article in *Newsweek*, and all of a sudden the phone rings."

"At four in the morning?"

"At four in the morning. It scared me out of my wits," Anne said, fighting fatigue, having her usual early gossip session with Carol Trager, a free-lance commercial artist who was doing brochures for Stellar Motors. They were gulping coffee in Anne's small, temporary office, surrounded by press releases, bulletin boards covered with notes and walls covered with pictures of the new jet-black FSR cars, direct from Bavaria, the pride of Stellar. Outside the small office was a large floor with rows of desks occupied by salesmen, copywriters, and technical service representatives, all part of the push for the FSR's big introduction to America.

"What'd he want?" Carol asked.

"He just wanted to find out if anything was wrong. He came in late and saw my light on."

"A gift from a merciful God," Carol said, her huge blue eyes lighting up the office. "I've got a single doctor living across my street, and he'd step over my body if he saw me dead. Count your blessings. This sounds like a live one. What's he like?''

"I've only met him a couple of times. He's good-looking, and just—you know—nice. I think he's the kind you could spend hours talking to. But I wonder why he comes in late so much."

Carol dropped her doughnut back onto her desk. "Hey look," she said, "if I were you, I wouldn't do too much wondering. You're looking to get something going. Here's a nice guy who cares. I mean, he didn't try to drop over at four A.M., did he?"

"Oh, no."

"And he doesn't seem to be a psychopathic sex fiend, does he?"

"Not so far."

"So he's a straight shooter. I say, go get him."

It was typical of Carol Trager, whose huge mass of bushy brunette hair overwhelmed her face. She was thirty, unmarried, with no prospects, and had an earthy manner that some found endearing, and others offensive. She was everyone's friend, but no one would assign her to diplomatic missions.

"He came into his house," Anne continued, "and didn't turn on a light for fifteen minutes. It was odd."

Carol put her head down on Anne's desk, spreading her mop of hair all over the surface, covering her ears with her hands. "I don't want to hear it," she said. "Annie, this is your problem. You're a worrier. That's why you can't sleep. I don't care what the shrink man says. So he didn't put the light on. So what? Does that bother you? Does it make him a bad person? Maybe he went to the john. Maybe he dropped down on his couch to get some winks. You want a private eye to check it out? Hey, I got a friend in the CIA. Want his number?"

"No," Anne replied, with a slight, nervous laugh, beginning to feel embarrassed by her hesitation. Of course, she understood *why* she worried. She'd been so burned by her marriage, so betrayed by a man she thought she knew, that suspicion now came naturally to her, far more naturally than acceptance or belief. And the insomnia made her even more wary. It made her weaker and more vulnerable. "I'll get to know him," she said. "Maybe he'll call again."

"Or maybe you'll call him," Carol said. "Look, it's done. Don't play 1950s' innocent maiden."

A messenger threw open the door, letting in the relentless clatter from the rows of people outside. He dropped a pile of papers on Anne's desk. "Herr Schultz wants these rewritten by noon," the teenage messenger announced, then turned and exited.

"Lovely," Anne mumbled. "I can hardly keep my head up and I've got to get these out by noon—extolling the virtues of a $10,000 car that they'll sell for $40,000."

"Well," Carol shrugged, "you know what FSR stands for, don't you?"

"No, I really don't," Anne said.

"For the stupid rich."

They both got a laugh out of that one, and Anne turned her chair back to her desk to resume work. "Better get started," she said.

"In more ways than one," Carol answered. "Hey, what's this love-machine neighbor of yours do?"

"For a living?"

"No, for his mother. Of course for a living."

"I never asked."

"Don't worry about it. He can afford a house in New Rochelle. He's not a part-time poet."

"I'll have him over," Anne said. "I'll find some excuse."

"Sure you will. Look, you barely just moved in. You're

getting to know the neighbors. What's more natural. Get to know him. Let it happen.''

Through the veil of her bloodshot eyes, Anne smiled, one of the few times Carol had seen such a full, enthusiastic smile. Of course Carol was right. Just let it happen. Get to know Mark Chaney. The questions will resolve themselves quickly. This could be the start of a rebirth, Anne knew. She felt a sudden charge of energy, a charge that, for the moment, overcame her fatigue. The phone call of the previous night rolled over and over in her mind, even to the point where she began to imagine that Chaney sounded far more interested than he actually had. The whole episode was some kind of heavenly sign, some signal, some turn of fortune. Just let it happen. How many women get a concerned call at 4:00 A.M. from a guy who seems to have everything?

She couldn't wait for her next encounter with Mark Chaney.

And neither could he.

3

Mark spun the Jaguar into the parking lot on Westchester Avenue in White Plains with all the confidence of the successful business executive that he was. It was almost funny, he thought, but he automatically listened for the thumping in the trunk that he'd heard the night before. And he made a mental note to get those blankets, so he would never hear that sound again. He zipped around the lot, tree-lined and surrounded by grass lawns, and pulled into parking space number one, with his name painted on the curb. Right next to him was Emil Welder's Mercedes 450SL in space number two. Emil didn't mind the distinction. There was an equality between the two men born of a burning past.

Mark got out of the car, retrieved his attaché from the spare-tire compartment, and started walking.

His office was in a glass building, one of six in a modern, idyllic complex that served White Plains. The "campus," as many of the people who worked there called it, did remind the visitor of a college. It was remarkably quiet, landscaped with a generous number of hills and walks, with virtually no litter anywhere. Chaney vastly preferred it to the clutter and noise of New York City, which seemed oppressive and threatening. Here he felt serene and in control, possibly for the first time in his twisted life.

He took the elevator to the third floor, entirely occupied by M.E., Inc., which stood for Mark and Emil, but which also symbolized the prevailing ethic of the decade. M.E., Inc. was a financial services firm, offering almost anyone the prospect of getting rich very quickly through investments in high-tech, coal mines, and Asian heavy-goods manufacturers. Mark and Emil had founded it in 1974, and both had become comfortable giving financial advice to the uninitiated and handling stock transactions. They had been shrewd enough to survive the stock market turmoil that began in October 1987 without major damage.

Mark swept into the carpeted, plush outer lobby, smiled a quick greeting to the receptionist, and rushed inside. He walked down a paneled corridor until he came to Emil Welder's office, as plush as the rest of the place, with a massive oak desk, red carpeting, and walls covered with reasonably good modern art.

Welder was at the desk. Overweight, breathing heavily, prematurely balding, he looked fifteen years older than Mark, although both were thirty-six.

Welder looked up. Both chins smiled. "Good work, baby," he said, in a voice raw from cigarettes.

"Thanks," Mark replied.

"I must've stayed up two hours after you called," Welder went on, glancing at his gold watch. "I don't think I've ever been happier. Jesus, I'm happy! Tell me, how'd he look?"

"About the same as he did when we were in school. A few more wrinkles, but the mean look."

"He was always mean," Welder said.

"He looked at me. He didn't even say hello. Can you believe that? Not even a simple hello."

Emil Welder shook his head in disgust. "Typical," he said. "The man had no warmth, no human feeling. You wonder how a guy like that got where he got." He and Mark understood each other, both living in their own world of dreams and petty resentments, a world they had made together, one they wanted to destroy together.

"Did he know what was happening?" Welder asked.

"At one point, I think."

"Tell me the whole thing. I want every detail. He say anything at all?"

"He didn't say a word."

"Not a word? Him? The mouth? I love it. Don't you love it, Mark? Was he scared?"

"I think in the last second, when he knew what was happening," Mark said, now sitting down in a roomy leather chair opposite Welder's desk. "Maybe he was just surprised. But when he saw what I had . . . yeah, he was scared."

"I hope he knew exactly what was going to happen," Welder said, a seething anger in his voice, the cigarette lungs almost gasping for air. "I hope he recognized you and remembered everything he did."

"I hope," Mark said.

"He at your house?"

"Yeah. I think he'll be good. Not too much damage. We can fix it."

"Have you seen the papers?" Welder asked, his face beaming with pride.

"No. He in there already?"

"He sure is. Page six, *New York Times*. Retired juvenile court judge disappears. Bloodstains outside his house. Don't you love it, Mark?"

"I love it," Mark said.

"They've even got a picture of the little wifey in distress. And they're wondering—get this—if there's going to be a ransom demand. Can you believe this? Who'd pay for that guy?"

"Amazing," Chaney said.

Welder suddenly frowned, his bushy eyebrows coming down like shades atop his watery eyes. "What about his gavel?"

"I checked. That court gives the judge his gavel when he retires. It must be in his house. I don't know if it's worth a break-in."

"I'd love to have that gavel," Welder said. "You remember how he rapped it when he sent us away? I'd love to have that exact gavel."

"Look, Emil," Chaney said, "I've got to give you a professional assessment. I want the gavel, too. But I don't know where he kept it. I mean, maybe it's in a safe. Maybe he gave it to his grandchildren. Who the hell knows? But it's not worth it."

Emil Welder leaned his 240-pound mass back in his chair and stared out the window, weighing Chaney's conclusion. "You're right," he said. "You're the one who's taking the chances. I wish I could do what you do, Mark. I get out of breath just yawning."

"I do it for both of us," Mark Chaney said. "And don't forget the planning we do, Emil. You're a brilliant planner. We're a team."

"They never understood how brilliant we were, did they, Mark?"

"No," Mark replied. "I think we were beyond them. All these people, like the judge, they were mediocre. The mediocre never understand genius. So they persecute the genius. They put him in jail or taunt him. It happened to us.''

"It happened to us," Emil echoed plaintively, staring out his window. "But genius always wins. All these people in school, in the courts, these people who robbed our youth, who put us in that institution, now they'll suffer. But they'll never understand.''

"No one understood Leopold and Loeb either," Mark said.

"We're so much like them, aren't we, Mark?"

"Yes," Mark answered. "And we'll kill together, like them, or we'll go down together..."

"Like them," Welder added.

He and Mark just smiled, their eyes locked on each other as if their minds were one, a psychotic partnership in the manufacture of death.

"How soon before the next chapter?" Emil asked.

"A few days. I've got all the information I need. I was in Philadelphia last week, and cased the house again. It'll be very easy.''

But Emil Welder looked into Mark's face and realized what he hadn't realized earlier—that Mark Chaney was troubled. Usually, when they discussed a new "project," Chaney would light up, become animated, practically act out what he planned to do, and whip open his attaché case to consult notes. But now he just sat there, as if something were tugging at the back of his mind and restraining him. "Mark, what's wrong?" Welder asked.

"I'm not sure," Mark answered. "We may have a problem.''

"What kind of problem?"

"I'm not sure of that either. There's this woman across the street..."

"Mark, you're not getting involved with a woman, are you? You promised not to do that until we finished everything."

"No, it has nothing to do with that, Emil. This is a woman who moved in three months ago. She's renting the house opposite mine. She's some kind of publicity person, and she's had a bad divorce. I don't know. Something like that. But whenever I come in at night after a project, she's looking through her window."

Welder's double chin began to quiver as a pale grimness came over him. "You sure she's looking at you, Mark?" he asked.

"At that hour? What else?"

"Maybe she's a night owl."

"No. I see her leaving early for work. Now, when I say work, I can't be exactly sure what it is. The publicity thing may be a cover. You know what I'm talking about."

"I'm afraid I do," Emil said. "Does she know you've found her out?"

"I don't think so. But I'm just guessing that she can't see me looking back. It worries me. Her house is rented. That worries me more. The police would rent a house for surveillance. They'd never buy it."

"Yeah, that's right."

"And it's the consistency. She's up so much. If I'd seen her once or twice, I wouldn't have thought much of it. But it seems to be all the time. Twice this week, when we didn't even have projects, I set my alarm for four A.M. so I could get up and check on her. Sure enough. Her light was on."

"Was she looking?"

"Occasionally she looked. My house was dark, though. There was nothing to see."

"Her light on?" Emil asked.

"Yes."

Now Emil shrugged, his whole suit moving with his massive shoulders. "Isn't that strange?"

"Why should it be strange?"

"If she was checking on you, wouldn't she do it from a dark house? Why would she attract attention by turning on the light?"

"I thought of that," Mark answered. "Maybe that's part of the cover. If her light was off, and I spotted her sneaking a look through a shade—maybe from the moon bouncing off her face—I'd have reason to be suspicious. Maybe she thinks that, with the light on, I'd assume she was one of those night people."

"Yeah, maybe."

"I looked through her window, Emil. I saw a camera with a telephoto lens. Professional equipment. But there were no pictures on the wall—not what I'd expect from someone with a camera like that."

"Mark," Emil asked, "you think we made a mistake somewhere?"

Chaney got up and started to pace nervously, his rough, good looks marred by the worry in his face. "No," he said. "We made no mistakes. But maybe someone found out."

"Who?"

"The police. Maybe a private person. She could be an investigator. Look, this can't be a coincidence. *That* house, right across the street, rented, a woman moving in just after we started these projects, with a long-lens camera, up at night when I come in."

"Any sign your house has been broken into?"

"No. And everything is locked up. I'd know if the locks were touched."

"Is it possible," Emil asked, "that she's just a snoop? Maybe she was up a few times, saw you come in, and wonders about you. Maybe she *likes* you. Some women get that way, you know."

"So?" Mark asked. "What if she *is* just a snoop? After a while, she'll begin to wonder. How many excuses can I give her? Business trips? Parties? Emil, I don't like this. She's watching me."

"You want to stop our project?"

"No. I'll never stop. I'll never stop until we finish what we started. But I've got to deal with her."

"Ideas, Mark?" Emil smiled. Mark knew that smile, knew what it signaled. He had seen that smile just before they discussed their first project.

"I know what you're thinking," Mark said. "She'd probably look pretty good in my freezer. It's easy. It's quick. I could get into her house before she got home and take care of things. But it's no good."

"Why?"

"It would bring attention to the neighborhood. If she disappeared, I'd be questioned by the police just because of where I lived. Did you see anyone? Did you hear her argue? Did anything suspicious happen on the block? I don't want the attention. It's the last thing we want."

"Well reasoned."

"And if she *is* working for the police, she's the last one I'd want to eliminate. That would clinch it for them."

"True again," Emil said. "All right. Analysis and solution?" It was a typical Emil Welder question, and typical of the pair. After all, they had M.B.A.'s, and this was no different from analyzing a business problem.

"Do nothing," Chaney replied. "Always the first possibility in a business crisis. I'll watch her, the same way she's watching me. I'll get to know her, maybe develop a relationship with her, lead her on. Sooner or later she'll make a mistake and let on what she's doing. I'll find out."

"I don't know," Emil said.

"You doubting me?" It was a rare flash of anger between them.

"Not doubting," Emil said. "But you convinced me that she's watching you. *Watching* you. And all you're going to do is go out on some dates?"

"Emil," Mark replied, "trust me. Just trust me, especially with women. But if I decide she has to die, even if I take some heat, she dies. There are ways. Nothing will stop us. Trust me."

Anne took an extended lunch hour to go to the Bradshaw Sleep Clinic on East Thirty-first Street, right near Bellevue Hospital. The clinic was housed in the two lower floors of a brownstone, with Dr. Bradshaw, his wife, and four-year-old son occupying the upper two floors. The clinic had established a national reputation for dealing with sleep problems, especially insomnia. Anne had always been amused at the photograph that hung just inside the front door: a picture of President Reagan snoozing while Pope John Paul II was making a speech. The caption underneath read, "Sleep overcomes all."

Cecil Bradshaw was thirty-six, of average height, with a bushy beard and thick horn-rimmed glasses that gave him a forbidding, scholarly appearance. He had graduated in the top one percent of his class from Harvard Medical School and was already a full professor at New York University. Students feared his brutal exams and his severe written appraisals of their work. But in his own clinic he was remarkably gentle and soft. Here he spoke almost in a whisper, as if he was around sleeping people, or people who wished they were sleeping. And he usually was.

He met Anne in his small, unimposing office stuck at the back of the brownstone, with one tiny window overlooking a garden. His desk was cluttered with charts that followed the brain waves, eye movements, and chin-muscle activity of patients who'd actually slept at the clinic to be evaluated. On the walls were photographs of some of those patients, faces not shown, sleeping in the clinic, sensors placed all over their bodies to record every nuance of activity.

"You have your sleep-wake diary?" Bradshaw asked Anne, his voice so low she hardly heard him.

"Yes," Anne replied, handing over a little notepad that contained everything about her sleep times, waking times, and sleeplessness for the past week. It also contained a record of all caffeine-containing beverages she had consumed during the same period.

Bradshaw studied the diary only briefly. "Same old story," he said. "Another bad week."

"Yeah, rotten," Anne said.

"But I see you're staying away from sleeping pills. That's good."

"I'm trying to do exactly what you say."

"Did anything happen in the last week to make things worse?" Bradshaw asked. "Stress at work?"

"There's stress at work," Anne reported, "but it's related to my being so tired all the time. They pile it on, and I'm too exhausted to do it quickly."

"Have you discussed this with the management?"

"I'm free-lance. Expendable. You don't discuss problems like that."

"I see. All right, have you been taking any kind of medication?"

"No. Well, I did take two aspirin for a headache."

"But nothing else?"

"No."

"Have you had any symptoms other than sleeplessness? Sore throat? Fever?"

"No," Anne replied. "I'm the picture of worn-out health."

Bradshaw just smiled at the remark. "Have there been any unusual events? Has your former husband been in contact? Deaths in the family? Social problems?"

"No. Nothing like that."

"OK," Bradshaw said. "Sounds uneventful. Now, I have the results of your neurological tests, and they're negative, as I'd expected. Now, when you slept here—and I think we've gone over this—we did a polygraph of your night's sleep. It's about eighteen hundred feet long, by the way, and I've had it reviewed by several physicians. There's really nothing in it to reveal why you're having this bout with insomnia. And the chemical tests are negative. I thought it might be fatigue caused by a thyroid problem or low blood sugar. But we've ruled that out too. Look, this isn't physical. I'm convinced you're going through a period of depression caused entirely by your divorce."

"Well, I can't undo the divorce," Anne said.

"No, but you can get past it. Maybe some psychological counseling will help. It's up to you."

"I usually don't feel comfortable with shrink stuff. I'm hoping time will take care of this."

"The loss of sleep can cause physical damage before time takes care, Anne. Think about that. But, look, if psychiatry doesn't make you comfortable, what about some time off? A vacation? Change of scenery? A..." He smiled. Anne could read his thoughts.

"A man?"

"I don't like to impose."

"You're right. A new relationship would help. I know myself, and I know that's at least part of the answer. It's also possible." And Anne broke out in a broad smile.

"Oh? Tell me."

"There's someone in my neighborhood. I'm getting to know him. He's, uh, attractive . . . in the old-fashioned way. And, miracle of miracles, I *think* he's interested. I mean, he helped me start my car. He called me last night—in the *middle* of the night—when he saw my light on . . . just out of concern."

"Hey, terrific. Why was he up that late?"

"Business, I think. I guess he comes in late from trips."

"Anne, you pursue this," Bradshaw ordered. "Sounds like a great, caring guy. Someone who'd call at that hour, just to find out about you . . . not too many around like that. This is very good news. Now, you check with me in about a week. I have the feeling there'll be progress. I just have that feeling."

And so did Anne.

She suddenly felt new energy, new spirit. Bradshaw was encouraging her. Carol was encouraging her. She kept hearing Mark Chaney's soothing voice. She knew quality when she found it.

A new life was beginning.

4
—

Anne's home phone rang at 8:06 P.M.

"Hi," the caller said.

At first, maybe because Anne was caught off guard, the voice didn't register. "Uh, hi," she replied.

"Mark Chaney," the voice said. "Remember?"

Remember? How could she forget? "Mark!" she exclaimed. "Sorry I didn't recognize—"

"People sound different in the middle of the night," Chaney said, then regretted that he'd said it. Why emphasize his knowledge of the night?

"Yeah, I guess they do."

"The reason I called was . . . well, we're neighbors, and I thought, maybe, you'd like to drop by for a munch, or a drink, or some heavy talk."

Anne couldn't believe this was happening. It *was* heaven-sent. She loved Mark's modesty, the respect in the way he'd asked her. "Sure," she said. "We've got something in common."

"Oh?" Chaney asked. "What's that?"

"We both like staying up nights."

There were a few moments of awkward silence as Chaney calculated how to respond. What was she saying? Was she accidentally slipping something? "Professional liability," he laughed. "How about an hour from now?"

"I'll clear my desk." Anne's heart was pounding as the conversation ended. Yes, she was still fighting fatigue. Her eyes were burning, her shoulder muscles a mass of ache. She knew she could never look her best because exhaustion was painted all over her face. But now she had a reason for enduring, for going all out. She changed into an informal, yet alluring dress and patched herself up as well as she could. And she debated whether to bring something over to Chaney. Maybe he'd like some fruit. Ice cream. Something. But she hardly knew him and thought it might look a little prissy, a little too possessive. Careful, Anne told herself. Don't destroy this chance. Don't go barging in and scaring him away.

Mark Chaney also prepared. First, he checked to make sure there was no evidence of the projects he and Emil were carrying out. If Anne were watching him, checking on him, she'd have her eyes all over his house. If he got distracted—by a phone call, for example—she might even search drawers. He put the notes for his upcoming "Philadelphia project" in a wall safe. He checked the locks to his basement but then removed one because two locks on a basement door looked funny. He even rehearsed a cover story in case Anne asked why there were *any* locks on a basement door. Some valuable business papers stored down there, he'd say.

He shaved and fixed himself up. If he were going to develop a relationship with her, he knew he had to be convincing, to do everything normal men did.

Then he turned on a voice-activated tape recorder that was hidden behind a bookcase. He wanted to be able to study every word Anne uttered, and to have Emil study the tape if he had to.

Both of them waited.

A few minutes before the appointed time Chaney glanced out his window to see the silhouette of Anne in her living room, raising her left arm to look at her watch. And then she got up smartly, more smartly than an insomniac usually did. She walked to her front door and opened it. Chaney moved back from his window, but not without first noticing that Anne, as usual, had left her Oldsmobile in the driveway. It was accessible. Chaney knew about cars, about how to make things happen to them. He made a mental note.

No one was going to cross him again, not without paying the price that he and Emil should have extracted years ago.

Anne crossed the street and rang Chaney's bell. He came quickly to the door and opened it with a broad smile.

"Welcome," he said. "We should've done this before."

"And it should've been me who invited *you*," Anne replied, sweeping in. "What a delightful house."

"Oh, thanks. That's right, you've never seen it from the inside. I've got a cousin with great taste. I'll have to give her credit for the decorating."

"You'll also have to give me her name," Anne said.

"Why don't you sit down," Chaney told her. "Make yourself at home. I'm glad I have the night free. The way business has been—"

"What kind of business is it?" Anne asked, then ground her teeth. Certainly forward, wasn't she? "Uh, maybe I shouldn't ask."

"Why not? It's no secret. I'm in financial services." He tried to give the impression that he was delighted Anne asked. "I have an old friend, and we formed this company some years ago. We research unusual investments and handle the stock transactions for our clients. It's very stimulating, but it can get crazy, especially when one of our recommendations goes wrong. That's when I'm out late, having crisis meetings and keeping clients happy. There's been a lot of that recently. Maybe you've noticed my late-night excursions. Oh, uh, something to drink?"

"Just a soft drink, if you don't mind."

"Not at all. That's what I'm having." He wanted to be sure his mind was absolutely clear for this evening. He went to a small bar at one end of the living room and fixed the drinks, watching Anne out of the corner of his eye. Sure, she was looking around... very carefully. Of course, it could be the curiosity of a new neighbor. The living room *was* attractive—with massive couches facing each other and antique furniture tastefully placed—but those eyes of hers seemed to catch everything.

"I forgot the ice," Mark said with an embarrassed laugh.

He had it all planned. He walked into the kitchen, listening for any sign that Anne was getting up to look further. There wasn't any. She was sitting in place. But did that really mean anything? Maybe she was just shrewd, not wanting to make suspicious noises.

He returned with the ice. "You know," he said, "I don't think you mentioned what *you* do."

"Oh, I'm a publicity writer," Anne replied, feeling an extra tinge of nervousness at the question, almost as if it were a college interview. "You know, public relations."

"Very interesting work," Chaney said, sitting down opposite Anne. "I kind of thought of going into that at one time. You work for a firm?"

"No, I'm free-lance."

Chaney chewed over that answer. He didn't like it. A

free-lance publicity writer had no ties to any existing organi-
zation. It was a wonderful cover for police work, or private
investigation. "In other words," he said, "you have your
own business."

"Yes. I work out of my house, ... which is why you
sometimes see me up late at night. Right now I'm doing an
assignment for the firm that imports the new FSR cars. I'm
enjoying it."

"I see. Well," Chaney said, "we're both entrepreneurs. I
know how tough it is. Look, I don't mean to intrude, but if
you ever need any financial advice, please don't hesitate."

"That's very kind of you."

"Come on, no it isn't. Sometimes even we, uh, captains
of industry need a shoulder to cry on."

It was touching, Anne thought. Again there was that
genuineness. Even after a few minutes she felt a warmth
radiating from Mark. Obviously, he was the protective type,
and his broad, Kennedyesque smile seemed to melt everything in its path.

"How long have you been at it?" he asked.

"Only three years. I had a full-time job up to then. Oh,
by the way, I was married before." Again, she mentally
kicked herself. Why was *that* necessary to say? Did she feel
compelled to admit her entire past, to give him the full
statement of her assets, liabilities, and previous mileage?

"Was your husband in the same business?" Chaney
asked, not missing a beat.

"No," Anne replied and went no further. "I'd love to
hear more about *your* work," she said, sounding as awkward as she felt.

There she goes, changing the subject, Chaney thought.
She doesn't want too many questions. She brought up her
former husband because she didn't like to be asked about

what she was doing now. He felt increasingly sure that his suspicions were valid.

"It's exciting work," Chaney said.

"I'll bet."

"My partner and I search out those promising new companies that are off the beaten path. We've even arranged the financing of companies, with our clients' money—and some of ours. We have to be careful, especially with all the bumps in the economy."

"I can see why you come in at all hours. It must be grueling."

"I guess so. I go to other cities. Very grueling."

"Why don't you just stay over?"

Chaney wasn't ready for the question. He'd never thought she'd ask anything like that. But she was obviously probing. "I guess I'm just a home-loving type," he answered. "I've never been one for hotels."

"But you must be exhausted the next day."

"Well, you know, when you're the boss, you come in anytime. So, if I have a late night, I make up the sleep the next morning. Refill?"

"No, I'm fine," Anne replied. She wondered if she were being too inquisitive, but she'd always had this desire to know everything about a man before beginning a serious relationship. She was obsessed with her one burning experience, her marriage and divorce, and didn't want to relive it.

"I was wondering about *your* nights," Chaney said. "When you're up late, what does that do to your mornings?"

"A lot," Anne admitted. "We free-lancers really can't come in late. When you're on assignment it's a job like any other. I get tired. *Very*."

"Rearrange your schedule."

"Maybe someday." Anne felt the tension inside her increase. She didn't want to admit that she was an insomniac. She *knew* that the insomnia was caused by depression, and no one wants to start a relationship with a depressive. She couldn't admit the truth to Mark, at least not yet.

"I'm surprised you do that to your health," Chaney said, standing up to get himself another Coke. "Can't you finish all your work in the early evening?"

"I try, but sometimes it doesn't get done."

"Then maybe you're becoming too successful. You may have to farm part of it out." Mark kept probing, dissatisfied with Anne's excuses for staying up so late, wondering why someone so intent on working those hours would waste time staring out the window.

"I've thought of that," Anne said, hating herself for being deceptive. "Maybe I'll do it, if I can afford it. Oh, by the way, I'd love to see the house."

"The house?"

"Sure," Anne said. "I like houses."

"Well, . . . of course." Chaney felt a thunderbolt go right through him. OK, maybe it was a compliment. People do ask to see other people's houses. But maybe she was interested in a lot more than architecture.

"I just think it's so elegant," Anne said. She really didn't think she was snooping. In fact, she thought she was being flattering.

"Thanks," Chaney said. No problem, he thought to himself, except for the basement. But the basement could be bypassed. "Why don't we begin right there, in the kitchen."

"Terrific."

Anne picked up her Coke and followed Mark into the kitchen, studying everything as she walked, especially a small painting of a Japanese garden.

"Lovely picture," she said.

"Oh, I'm glad you like it."

"Very much."

"My partner did that. He loves to paint. That garden is just outside a semiconductor company in Japan. We helped finance it."

"I see. Mixing art with commerce."

"Exactly."

The tour didn't take long. Chaney's was a ranch house with three bedrooms. It was tastefully done, but there wasn't anything that striking about it. Anne did the usual oohs and aahs, and she got the impression that Chaney was a fairly typical bachelor who lived below his means and simply didn't want to be bothered with a larger house.

Chaney watched Anne carefully during the tour. She didn't give away any secrets, and he couldn't detect her real purpose by her behavior. He was still looking for some slip.

Finally, after about ten minutes, they returned to the living room. "Lovely," Anne said. "But you didn't show me the basement."

Chaney laughed. "Why would you want to see the basement?"

"It's part of the house."

"It is? Funny, I never really thought of the basement as anything but a storage area, or where they put the oil burner, or dead bodies." He laughed, probing to see if she'd respond.

"Mine is finished," Anne said. "You could do a lot with a basement. May I see it?"

Now Chaney felt his guts tightening up. Sure, she knew something was going on down there. Why else would she ask? It wasn't normal. Whoever heard of someone with a basement fetish?

But how do you handle it without looking suspicious? "If

you want to see my regal basement," he said, "I'll be glad to show it to you." His mind raced, going through different strategies, rejecting them, knowing he'd have to come up with something fast.

Anne noticed his discomfort. Maybe she was annoying him. It would be just like her, she thought. Always pushing too hard. Maybe she should change the subject. But, before she could, Chaney was already walking.

"Right this way," Chaney told her and led her to the locked basement door.

Anne regarded the lock, a quizzical look forming on her face. "What have you got down there, the Mona Lisa?" she asked.

Chaney attempted a little laugh. "I store some valuable records in the basement. With the robbery rate around here . . ."

"I know what you mean."

Casually, having passed that hurdle, Chaney started opening the combination lock. He took his time, his mind still flowing with ideas for avoiding a major flap. Finally, the lock snapped open. "There we are," he said. "Welcome to the crown jewels." He opened the door and flipped on the basement light. A fear jolted him: would she *smell* anything? He wondered if he'd become oblivious to the smell of the merchandise.

They started down the stairs. Now he tried but couldn't smell anything unusual, and he doubted that she could.

At the bottom, Chaney surveyed the area. "Just a basement," he said. "Oil burner over there. Washing machine. Dryer. No, I don't really do my own wash."

"And a freezer," Anne said.

"I love steaks."

Stupid, Chaney thought. He'd never bothered to put a lock

on the freezer. A cheap two-dollar lock would be worth a million right now. "Seen enough?" he asked.

Anne didn't answer. Instead, she walked over toward the freezer. My God, Chaney thought, she was going to open it . . . those big green bags . . . she'd wonder, she'd find out.

But she veered away.

She walked toward the other padlocked door, leading to the finished portion of the basement. "Den?" she asked.

"Uh, no," Chaney replied. "That's the storage, which is why I've got a lock on there too."

"Oh. Well, I don't want to bother you with more locks."

She turned to the staircase.

They walked back upstairs, the pounding in Chaney's chest reduced to a minor engine knock.

Either Anne didn't know what was going on in the basement, or didn't care to let on, Mark reasoned. He still couldn't read her. If she were a pro, working with the police, she was the best he'd ever seen.

They returned to the living room after Chaney relatched the lock on the basement door. New ideas began forming in his head, ideas that would help him uncover the motives of this woman who spied on him every time he came in late.

"Do you travel much?" Chaney asked, as he poured himself another drink.

"Occasionally," Anne said. "I've never been a big fan of traveling on business, but sometimes it's necessary. I'm debating whether to go on a trip in the next couple of weeks."

"Oh?"

"The car company wants to unveil one of its new models in Detroit—you know, do it right in the heart of our auto industry, to show the contrast."

"Shrewd move," Chaney said.

"And they invited me to come along and help their regular publicity staff."

"Do it."

"You think I should?"

"Why not? That's great experience for you. If you don't do it, someone else might slip right into your job. I see it happen every day."

"Maybe I will. I have a cat. I hate to put him in a kennel."

"I'll take the cat," Chaney said.

"Would you?"

Chaney smiled, giving it everything he had. He knew what that smile, those clear eyes, could accomplish. "I would for *you*," he replied.

Anne loved the sound of that. She'd never heard it once in her marriage. "Thank you," she said. "I appreciate that so much. People don't understand how animal lovers feel."

But Chaney wondered what this was all about. Why was she really traveling?

"You just give me a day's notice," Chaney said.

"That would be wonderful."

"I'll be happy to watch your house, too," Chaney went on. Already, a plan was becoming clear to him. "Make sure you leave on some lights and lock everything. Do you have any kind of alarm system?"

"No, I never looked into that."

"Well, it might be a good idea. But, it can wait until after this trip. I'll tell you, this block has been fairly lucky. Oh, make sure to leave your car out. Let them think someone's home."

"Yeah, they have a lot to be afraid of in me," Anne said.

They both laughed. Anne could feel the intimacy growing between them after only an hour together. Yes, he *liked* her. He really did.

Chaney sensed that she was trying to get him involved, throw him off guard. He saw the danger and resisted it. He *would* pursue her relentlessly, even drawing her into his romantic orbit.

But romance wasn't on his agenda.

Murder, the bottom line, had been penciled in.

5

—

"It's no good," Chaney said, pacing up and down in Welder's office, his Dunhill jacket off, his gold cufflinks glistening in the morning sun that streamed in through the windows. "First, that rented house. I didn't get the feeling she makes too much money. How can she afford that house? The place has to go for $1,800 a month."

"Family money?" Welder asked.

"Maybe, but I wouldn't count on it."

"Or maybe her husband is picking up part of the tab. It could have been part of the divorce."

"I still don't like it," Chaney said. "Rentals are temporary. I don't like temporary. And then I found out she's free-lance. There's a cover for you. No long-term relationships. And the company she's working for is European."

"So?" Welder asked.

"Foreign companies can be pressured by American authorities. They may have asked these people to put her on their payroll. Foreign companies like an easy time here. Look, it's all fitting together. She's watching me. Emil.

47

She's *watching* me. It's the same story—there's always someone chasing us. They won't leave us alone.''

"You're not quitting, are you?" Welder asked, trying to get to his overburdened feet to emphasize the point and failing, flopping back down in his chair with a thud, gasping for breath.

Chaney just stared at him, at once wounded at the suggestion, yet defiant. Even among psychotics there is a fear of being shamed. Neither Mark nor Emil ever wanted to show weakness before the other. "I've told you before, Emil, I won't stop until our work is done," Mark said firmly, "until every last one of them is in my basement. But I've got to watch her too. I've got to find out everything about her. Funny, she acts like she's interested in me."

"Look out for that," Welder shot back, almost as if he were afraid Mark could be flattered. "That's how women get your guard down."

"This one won't have any effect on me," Mark said, again seeking Emil's approval. "By the way, she's going on a trip."

"So?"

"It provides an opportunity." Mark began to smile. "Especially since I'm watching her house. Houses reveal everything, don't they, Emil?"

"I follow you," Welder said.

Both men spun their fantasies, thoroughly convinced they were on to something. There was simply too much about Anne that was suspicious—starting with her late-night spying and continuing through her free-lance status, her rented house, the long-lens camera in her kitchen, even the enthusiasm with which she dropped everything to go to Chaney's place. And then there was her whole demeanor—always asking questions, always wanting to know more. Add to that the belief of Mark Chaney and Emil Welder that enemies were lurking in every shadow, and the mind-set was complete.

"What if she's serious trouble?" Welder finally asked, lighting up a cigarette and blowing out so much smoke that he was engulfed in mist within a few seconds. He coughed and heaved before he could get out his next words, wiping his brow with a handkerchief as sweat beads began to form. "I mean, Mark, what if you find out she could really hurt us?"

"Then we may have to take heat," Mark said.

"How much heat?"

"Much heat—even if the police start asking questions once they hear she's disappeared. I don't want that. I told you. But it may come to it. Or . . . wait a second. Wait a *second*."

"Yeah?"

"There's another way. She's had this divorce. I know that from the neighbors. She didn't talk much about it last night, but people with divorces go through bad periods. Depressed. Angry. Sometimes they . . . can't handle it."

"And they commit suicide," Welder said, his multiple chins and generous cheeks dissolving into a snide smile.

"Why not? 'She was confused,' I'd tell the cops. 'I tried to talk reason to her, to develop a relationship. But all she could talk about was her divorce. We went out, maybe to a park on top of the Jersey Palisades. When I wasn't looking, she. . . . It was all too terrible.' " Now he burst into laughter, and Welder loved it. He loved it when Mark laughed, because it meant he was solving a problem.

"Wonderful," Welder said. "But that would work only if she were a lone wolf, somebody just snooping after you. If she's working for the police, or a private eye, she's already briefing them. They'd never believe she was a suicide."

"Oh, I don't know," Chaney answered. "Actually, there's

a high rate of mental distress in law enforcement. Didn't our lawyer try to prove that Detective Forsyth was looney tunes when he arrested us? Even if she's a cop, she *did* have that divorce. Cops get the blues."

"Yeah, they do," Emil conceded.

"I think I'll look at locations this week . . . after Philadelphia."

"Locations?"

"Suicide locations, where a woman like Anne Seibert might feel in the mood. We can handle her, Emil. No one escapes us anymore. Right?"

"Always right."

"I go to Philadelphia tonight," Chaney said.

"Are you sure you're ready?"

"I'm sure. And the weather is ready. There'll be thunderstorms . . . with plenty of lightning. It makes everything so perfect."

"You are talking about a prince," Carol Trager said, listening to Anne relate the events of the evening before. "You are talking about pure royalty, and I don't care if he lives in New Rochelle. He is some kind of foreign prince. May I kiss the hand of the princess?"

"You really think I hit a home run, don't you?" Anne asked. They were munching on breakfast rolls, in Carol's little cubicle this time, while the staff of Stellar Motors filtered in for the morning's efforts at selling a car to the idiot rich that most Europeans regarded as barely average.

"You're already in the World Series," Carol answered. "I mean, the man asks you over, gives you the house tour, volunteers to watch your house *and* take your little kitty while you go to Detroit. What is he, a frustrated priest?"

"Almost," Anne replied. "I've got to say it—he may be the answer to a not-so-young-girl's dreams."

"And of course, you're going to find something to worry about, aren't you? I know, he parts his hair on the wrong side. Must be a psychological problem. Correct?"

"Incorrect," Anne answered, barely able to contain her laughter. "I have no doubts about the guy. He's perfectly normal, very courteous . . . and he seems balanced."

"What means that?" Carol asked, slurping her coffee and glancing around to make sure none of the bosses were coming.

"Well, after my former husband, I don't want any more lunatics. You don't know what it's like to live with a violent man, to look into those eyes when they catch fire and know what he might do. This man—Mark—he seems so calm. I mean, he's got a high-pressure job, but I don't think he takes it home."

"Aren't too many like that."

"He wasn't jumpy or defensive. No matter what we talked about, no matter what I asked him, he seemed so serene. He must have had a very happy childhood."

"Incredible. I'm putting in for maid of honor right now."

"I only found one thing strange. . . ."

"Oh, here we go."

"No, I'm sure it's nothing. But, he was telling me how late he sometimes works, how people constantly harass him because he's involved with their investments, how they call him at home all the time. . . . But it was funny, the phone never rang while I was there."

Carol laughed, burying her head in her hands, muffling the laugh so the troops outside couldn't hear. "I thought you were going to say he wore polka-dot miniskirts," Carol said. "Honey, did you ever consider that he might have an unlisted number?"

"It's in the book," Anne replied.

"OK, did you ever consider that he's got an answering

machine, and that he turned off the phone ringer just before you came? If he was hoping for some romance, he sure wasn't waiting for Ma Bell.''

"Well, maybe that was it," Anne said.

"Amazing how I settle all your little fears, isn't it? I oughta charge. Say, when you got back home last night, . . . did you sleep?''

"Like a baby.''

"Then this is it, kid. Any man who can do that for you has got to be the find of your life.''

"I just hope I don't ruin it," Anne said.

"You won't. Don't worry.''

"Oh, I'll worry.''

At that moment the phone rang in Anne's office next door. "Trouble," she said, expecting a business call, possibly from one of the automotive trade publications. She sauntered into her office, Carol Trager following with the coffee and rolls. Anne picked up.

"Anne Seibert, publicity.''

"Hello, Anne.''

"Well, hi,'' Anne answered. She gestured to Carol that it was Chaney on the other end. "To what do I owe this pleasure?''

"Oh, it's not such a pleasure,'' Chaney said. "I just thought I'd call and find out how things were.''

"I'm glad you phoned,'' Anne said.

She wouldn't have been if she knew the real reason for Chaney's call. He was beginning to move in on her, launching a detailed probe to find out what she was up to. "You dropped your lipstick in my living room," he told her. "I'll leave it in your mailbox.''

"Oh, I'm sorry. Thanks.''

"I guess you didn't have much work last night.''

"Oh?''

"I looked out. Your light was off."

For a moment, Anne hesitated. Again, he was getting close to her insomnia. Did he suspect there was something wrong with her? Or was it an innocent question? "You're right," she said. "A light load yesterday. I'm feeling terrific."

"Great. Look, I'd love to get together with you again," Chaney said. "Maybe something a little more exciting next time. Would you?"

"Sure, love to," Anne answered, gesturing wildly to Carol that things were clicking.

"I'll be out of town for the rest of the day, back late tonight. What about Sunday?"

"Sunday's perfect."

"I'll call. We'll set up a time."

"Terrific," Anne said. "Oh, where you going tonight?"

"Albany," Chaney answered, lying all the way. "I've got clients there."

"I still don't see why you don't stay over."

"A man does what he must do. You'll probably hear me pulling in at some ungodly hour. Oh, there's my other phone. Talk to you before Sunday. Bye . . . Annie."

"Right. Bye . . . Mark."

Their conversation ended. Anne was in another world. "You won't believe it," she told Carol. "You just won't believe it."

Chaney commonly used private detectives to check out the management of companies, financial backers, and even potential employees of M.E., Inc. He'd already asked one of his investigators to check out Anne Seibert, explaining that he might want to hire her to do some publicity. He'd asked for a background check, with emphasis on any personal activities that might embarrass the Chaney/Welder firm.

That report had been on his desk even as he spoke with Anne by phone. Now he studied it carefully, watching for any nuance, any indication that the surface facts might only be window dressing:

> CLIENT: M.E., Inc.
> SUBJECT: Seibert, Anne
> INVESTIGATOR: Lisa
>
> Subject person was investigated from public documents, court records, official papers and was personally surveilled by the above-named investigator. Investigation confirms that subject is self-employed as a publicity writer and works and has worked for numerous firms in and around New York City. Investigation also confirms that subject has been married once and divorced. Former husband was judged by medical authorities to be mentally unstable and occasionally violent. Subject expressed fear of husband in court testimony.

Afraid of violent men, Chaney mused. At first he thought this was almost humorous. *He* was getting close to a woman who feared violent men. Ironic, he thought. He read on:

> Subject has filed two brutality complaints against husband. Husband in turn has charged her with adultery and mental cruelty. Charges against her dismissed by court. Interview with friendly business associate of subject indicates subject has suffered bouts of depression since divorce. Under medical treatment, precise nature of which we were unable to determine.

* * *

A nut case? Chaney wondered. Anne had more of a background than he'd imagined. In a way, he almost sympathized with her. He and Emil were victims, weren't they? But his sympathy faded as he read on and came to something intriguing:

> Subject works intermittently as a volunteer for a group that assists abused wives. She has written articles on violent men for said group.

True, she'd lived with a violent man, and so it was logical that she'd join such a group. But maybe she also had suspicions about men—virtually *all* men—and was venting those suspicions on him. Maybe she thought, or sensed, that there was something wrong with him.

Or maybe she knew something about his past.

And there was the writing. Of course. Anne Seibert was a journalist by training. Was she gathering information for some kind of exposé? He would have to add this to all his other concerns about her.

And the report said something else:

> Subject admitted to New York Hospital Payne-Whitney Psychiatric Clinic during divorce proceedings for treatment of nervous disorder.

What was Chaney dealing with?

He had to know.

Sitting in his regal office, decorated with Persian rugs and pieces of original sculpture, he slapped the report down on his desk and reached for his gold-plated phone. He called the home number for "Lisa," the investigator who'd written the report on Anne Seibert. His private eye always slept till noon at the earliest, and Chaney had regularly woken her up in the morning with questions.

The phone rang twelve times, par for the course, Chaney knew. Finally, someone picked up and answered.

"Lisa here," came the voice. The investigator referred to herself only as Lisa. Chaney never even knew her last name, making out the checks to Lisa, Inc. He knew Lisa to be in her fifties, smallish, bookish, more like a librarian than an investigator, but someone who carried a modified submachine gun in the trunk of her Subaru.

"Mark Chaney," he replied. "Wake you up?"

"Yes," Lisa answered. "Very rude. What do you want, Mark?"

"I'm reading your report on Anne Seibert," Chaney said. "Very interesting."

"I've seen better," Lisa answered, cuddled up under her pink silk sheets.

"I don't want a book review," Chaney told her. "Just tell me if you think I should hire her . . . and why."

"How would I know? She has a reputation for competence. A detail person. A worrier. You get to that part of the report yet?"

"No."

"I'll fill you in. She always gets the job done, no matter what it takes. Went to the Medill School of Journalism at Northwestern. They thought a lot of her."

"Does she stay on the right side of the law? That's important to us here, in financial services."

Lisa laughed. "Yeah, I know how important the law is to you money guys. Great reverence." She laughed again. "Yeah, she stays on the right side. She's written articles on family cops—you know, the ones who break up domestic disputes."

"So she has contact with the police."

"If you call that contact. I think she did those articles in Chicago, not here."

"I see. All right. I'll consider her. I may ask you for more."

"You write the checks, I get the facts." And Lisa hung up without another word.

Chaney put down the phone. With each piece of information, Anne Seibert became more fascinating. He'd always fought the idea of imagining things. Like many disturbed people, he *knew* he had problems. But how could he be imagining? She *did* spy on him. That was a fact.

He got up and started pacing his office, shutting the door so no one would bother him. He gazed out the window toward New York City, toward Anne, his mind ablaze with unanswered questions and a growing anxiety. Was someone closing in on his and Emil's ugly little secret?

Was she a police spy? A petty snoop? A psychotic who stayed up nights?

She could be any one of those things. But she *had* to be one of them.

He would find out which one.

After Philadelphia.

After the thunderstorms.

6

Chaney didn't go to Philadelphia for brotherly love. He went, after a dozen previous trips over a period of a year, to perform a sacred act of vengeance and bring home a prize. He traveled down the New Jersey Turnpike in the midst of a heavy downpour, accompanied by the rhythm of his windshield wipers and the soft whine of the radial tires. His mind drifted back to the source of this mission, to a suburban high school in New York, to Peter Riley, its principal.

Peter Riley. The very name sent waves of loathing through Mark Chaney's frame. He could recall every word Riley had spoken as he and Emil stood before him, stood before that massive wooden desk with the glass top, and the American flag on a pole behind it.

"You're scum," Riley had said. "I'm kicking you out of this school and turning you over to the police. They'll send you away. Maybe you'll die. Maybe they'll kill you there. As long as we're rid of you!''

The other kids could hear Riley shouting all the way down the hall. He always had such warmth, such understanding. He actually announced Emil's and Mark's names on the public address system when they were expelled, and later he announced, with obvious satisfaction, that they'd been sent to a juvenile detention center.

Mark recalled the humiliation.

He recalled how his parents cried, how the neighbors shunned them, how they had to sell their house and leave town.

All over a couple of robberies in the school hallways, the roughing up of a teacher, and the firing of a rifle bullet through a school window during class.

Peter Riley had never understood teenagers, and now Peter Riley would have to pay the price.

Last laugh, Mark thought to himself. *He* was driving a maroon Jaguar XJ6 with genuine leather upholstery. Riley was still driving that old Datsun. Chaney gunned his car's engine to pass a slower motorist, increasing his feeling of power and superiority over the high-school principal who'd caused him and Emil so much trouble.

"You boys think you could get away with this?" he'd asked, in that high-pitched, phony-scholarly way. "Think you can run the school? Well, you can't. I know your kind. You're bums.''

Now Chaney headed off the turnpike, toward Philadelphia itself. He quickly pulled into a Mobil station for fuel, making certain to choose a pump that was serviced by an attendant. No self-service. No leaving fingerprints anywhere.

"How do I get to New Hope?" he asked from behind tinted glasses.

The attendant shrugged. He'd never heard of New Hope,

but Chaney didn't care. He'd intentionally asked the attendant for directions to a place he wasn't going. He hoped the attendant would remember the question. If he was later asked if he'd seen a maroon Jaguar, the attendant might recall that, yes, he had, but that this one *wasn't* going to Philadelphia... where Peter Riley lived.

He was on his way again soon. He knew Riley's pattern. The old guy lived alone, his wife having died four years earlier. He went out every night about eight to get a late sandwich at a nearby chain restaurant. It must be the only entertainment in his dull life, Chaney mused.

Soon, Peter Riley would meet one of his prize pupils.

Anne felt it coming on.

She could almost predict when the insomnia was going to strike, and tonight she knew she was in for a bout. She tried to nap when she got home, but could barely close her eyes. She had hoped that the excitement of her new relationship with Mark Chaney would banish the insomnia forever, but now she knew that it was not to be. She glanced out the window at Mark's house, darkened in his absence, and only wished he'd come home.

She saw a police car go by, then slow down. The two patrolmen inside seemed to be eyeing Mark's house. Maybe he'd informed the police he'd be away and asked them to watch the place. It was like Mark to be thorough.

Anne had Dr. Bradshaw's home number and decided to give him a call. She had a new social situation, yet knew insomnia was coming, and maybe he had some suggestions. He'd always encouraged her to call him at home if need be.

Bradshaw picked up on the first ring. Anne quickly realized he whispered on the phone too, almost as quietly as he did in his office.

"Dr. Bradshaw here," he said.

"Anne Seibert, Dr. Bradshaw. I'm really sorry to bother you at home, but I just felt I had to talk."

"It's no bother, and I'm glad you called. Is there anything wrong, Anne?"

"Right and wrong," Anne answered. "Look, you sure this is a good time for you?"

"A perfect time. Now, you tell me what the problem is."

"Well," Anne replied, "it's about this man I met. I think I discussed him with you."

"Yes, I remember."

"Now, the first night I was with him, I came home and slept like a log . . ."

"Told you."

"Yeah, wait a second, doctor. He's away tonight, and I think it's coming on again. Now, is this going to happen every time he's away?"

"Very hard to answer, Anne. We don't know everything about the psychiatric aspects of insomnia. Obviously, you're not relaxed with him away. There may be apprehension. You might be worrying about his safety . . . or even if he's out with . . ."

Bradshaw didn't finish, but Anne instantly realized he was hitting a point. Of course she couldn't feel completely at ease. There really wasn't a relationship yet, even though she fantasized about one. And, yes, there was always a chance he had someone else. Crazy, but she really hadn't dealt with that consciously, as if she wanted to avoid it.

"I guess I am a little worried," she told Bradshaw.

"How deep is this relationship?" Bradshaw asked. "You mentioned something about the first time you were with him . . ."

Anne sighed. She really didn't want to admit it. "That was last night," she said.

There were a few moments' silence. Being very professional, Bradshaw would never laugh at a patient. Besides, he had seen this pattern before—the woman on the rebound, seeking a new passion. He understood it, and sympathized with it. "Look," he said, "try to relax as best you can. I'm still not going to allow you any drugs. It'll ruin everything. Just think about his coming back. Will he be away for long?"

"Oh, no. He's in Albany. He'll be in before dawn. He always does that."

"Well," Bradshaw said, "if I could read your subconscious, I'd say you're planning to be up when he comes home, and I don't see any remedy for that."

Anne laughed. She had always marveled at how incisive Bradshaw could be. He had it all nailed down, didn't he? "I'll do my best," she said. "And you're right. I'll probably be seeing him later."

"Good luck," Bradshaw said and hung up.

Now Anne felt a little foolish for even having called. She must've sounded so trivial, so worried about every little thing. But, if anything, her new connection with Mark had made her even more sensitive about her insomnia, even more determined to shake it before it destroyed her.

And yet, something new began to bother her. Yes, she enjoyed talking with Bradshaw, but now he had planted that seed she found so disturbing. Other women. Did they exist? What were they like? Were they attractive? Accomplished? How important were they?

Was Mark Chaney just toying with her?

The worrier worried. It was her curse.

Chaney cruised into the neighborhood where Peter Riley lived. He drove casually, as if he belonged there. He had considered using a rented car for these occasions, but had repeatedly rejected the idea. Going home with a rented car would attract neighborhood attention, and he would have to bring the car home to transfer cargo to his freezer. Besides, rented cars had to be rented from *somewhere*, and they always asked for a driver's license and credit cards. There'd be a record. Chaney depended on his professionalism, his ability not to draw notice. He could use his own car because no one would be given cause to remember it.

The rain came down heavily, each droplet splashing off the Jaguar with a little ping. Lightning flashed across the sky, revealing small houses and well-kept lawns. Seconds later came the thunder. Chaney loved nights like this for his project. He knew there was a risk that Riley might not go out in this kind of weather. But it was a risk he was prepared to take.

He glided past Riley's two-story brick house and saw the lights on. The old man was inside, his Datsun in the driveway. Chaney drove on to the little luncheonette where Riley religiously went every night. He parked about a block away, along a strip of stores that had closed hours before. And he waited. If everything went according to schedule, Peter Riley would be along in about ten minutes, no more than twenty. He checked the street signs once again to be sure he was legally parked. Attracting a traffic cop or meter maid would not be healthy.

On schedule, fourteen minutes later, Riley's Datsun appeared down the block, moving slowly through the rain. Riley parked right outside the luncheonette, locked his car doors, and went inside. He was slightly stooped from all the years of reading, and wore a black rubber raincoat, camper style, with a large rain hat. Under his arm, covered by a piece of plastic, was a copy of the *Philadelphia Inquirer.* Chaney watched as Riley greeted some of the patrons and sat at his favorite one-person table in the corner.

Chaney settled down for the wait, which he estimated

would be about forty minutes, unless one of Riley's friends entered the luncheonette. He tuned into an all-news radio station and heard a story about some Philadelphia stockbrokers indicted for fraud. He knew their names. He thought he'd met some of them once.

Riley was having his typical dinner: a hamburger with peas and a cup of coffee. It never varied. It had been the same in the school cafeteria when Riley ate with the students, another of his public-relations gimmicks, Chaney thought.

Occasionally, Riley would look out at the rain, his face wrinkled, his eyes squinty. Chaney hoped those eyes were still good enough to see clearly what was about to happen to him.

Anne tried to pass the time reading, but felt a grinding tension that made concentration impossible. It was still early in the evening, but she started to look out the window, hoping that Mark would return ahead of schedule. As she gazed at the house, she thought of the happy time she'd spent there and tried to imagine living in it with Mark.

Dreamily, she picked up her 35-mm camera and snapped some time exposures of Mark's house. Lit only by the streetlights, the house looked eerily serene in the rain, like something out of a horror story or an English mystery.

She glanced at her watch. It was 8:05 P.M.

After forty-seven minutes, Peter Riley left the luncheonette, and Chaney's heart sank, . . . for Riley left with a friend. The presence of another person would make the night's work impossible, and Chaney would have to return to New Rochelle a failure.

But, after speaking for a few moments outside, the friend left. Riley got back into his car.

All right, Chaney thought, this is it.

It was possible.

It could be done.

Riley started up the car and began moving down the street. Chaney followed, driving casually, attracting absolutely no attention. Riley turned a corner; Chaney came closer, now following no more than one hundred feet behind. The area had little traffic on clear nights, almost none tonight. Chaney literally looked through Riley's windshield to the area ahead, the area where, he knew, he had to make his long-planned, long-dreamed-of move. It was a darkened area, where the road was lined with several empty lots awaiting new construction.

Chaney accelerated, pulling up behind Riley's Datsun, then swerving to the left and pulling beside it. Chaney lowered his automatic right passenger window and gestured to Riley. Riley lowered his driver's window. Both cars stopped.

"Want something?" Riley asked.

"Yeah, I'm lost," Chaney replied. Before Riley could say anything more, Chaney jumped from his car and walked around to Riley, carrying a pencil and paper, as if to ask for directions. Riley looked annoyed at having been stopped like that, but he waited. Chaney approached him and raised the paper. "Say, I hate to bother you like this," he said, "but I can't find a street. I wonder if you could tell me where Deane Street is, and I'll draw a little map."

"Sure," Riley said. Always the civic hero, Chaney thought. Always helping a neighbor, just like he did in high school. "Deane Street is about three blocks down, past the second light. You have to—"

At that point Chaney snapped a pistol from his pocket and jammed it against Riley's skull. "Shut up," he said. "You do exactly what I say and you won't get hurt. This is a robbery. Nothing more—unless you make it more. Now, pull over to the curb, slowly. I'll walk with you. Try to gun your engine and get away, and they'll bury you in this car."

Riley, his face suddenly ashen with terror, yet glistening from the spray that came in the window, did exactly as he was told. When his car was at the side of the road, Chaney made him shut off the engine.

"Get into my car," Chaney ordered.

Riley, too frightened even to respond, left his car and hurriedly got into Chaney's. He was shaking with fear. Chaney slid into the driver's seat and locked all four doors by flipping a switch. Riley stared at Chaney's gun. "What are you doing with me?" he asked.

"Robbing you," Chaney responded with a smile. "I have my methods. We won't be going far."

"Just don't hurt me," Riley said. "I've got grandchildren. You can take anything. But just don't hurt me."

As Chaney gunned the engine and pulled ahead, his glance alternated between the road and Riley. Riley knew that any move would be fatal. At one point he looked down at the seat and realized it was covered with a green, plastic sheet. Why? He couldn't figure it out. Maybe it had something to do with the rain. Some people, maybe even highway robbers, have a fetish about keeping their cars clean.

Chaney drove to an industrial area nearby and stopped amid warehouses, all closed at this time of night. Then he flipped on the light in the car and turned menacingly toward Riley.

"You want my watch?" Riley said. "It's gold. A gift from my school. It's worth something."

Chaney didn't answer. He just kept staring into Riley's glasses.

"Look, I've got some money," Riley said. "I'll give you credit cards. Use them. I won't call anything in."

But Chaney just kept staring.

"Do I look familiar?" Chaney asked.

Riley was plainly startled by the question. What did this have to do with robbery? "No," he replied. "You don't look familiar."

"Look a little more carefully, . . . Dr. Riley."

"How did you know my name?" Riley asked.

"Look a little more carefully."

Riley stared but said nothing.

And then Chaney began to sing. "Hail Millwood High, we'll everlastingly be true . . ."

Riley squirmed in his seat. Even in his torment, he realized this had to be a former student. And now the face began to look familiar. It began to look frighteningly familiar. He was amazed he hadn't realized it before. How could he forget?

But hadn't this boy been locked up? Hadn't they put him away for attempted murder? He and his friend? Hadn't a psychiatrist recommended they throw away the key?

"What do you want, Mark?" Riley finally asked.

"Well," Chaney said, "I'm flattered, sir. You remember."

"Yes, I'm afraid I do. Why don't you put the gun away?"

"This isn't school, Dr. Riley," Chaney replied. "Don't tell me what to do."

"Mark, you'll never get away with this. You—"

"Who the hell are *you* to talk to me like that?" Mark asked indignantly. "Dr. Riley, you see this car? You see this Rolex watch? You see this Dunhill suit? I *earned* all this. I earned it 'cause I'm smart."

"I'm sure you are, Mark."

"Never thought I'd come this far, did you, Dr. Riley? You thought Emil and me would rot in that psychiatric hospital, didn't you? Well, they let us out. We conned the shrinks. It wasn't very hard. But we got hurt, Dr. Riley. We got hurt because of you and people like you.''

"I never tried to hurt you.''

"You sent us to the police.''

"That was my job!''

"You could've handled us.''

"No, I couldn't. You boys attacked a teacher. You attacked students. Nothing I did—''

"You gave us a record. Even today, we can't go back to the class reunion.''

"Look, Mark, I understand how you feel. That was years ago. You're better now. It's a pleasure to see you—''

"A pleasure? You think I believe you? You always lied to us. Emil told me that. You always thought you could put things over on us. You never paid for that.''

Now Riley began to draw away, squirming toward the passenger door. "What do you mean, paid?'' he asked.

Mark Chaney didn't answer. He simply continued to stare, Riley's face occasionally lit by lightning, the tension of the moment magnified by the thunderclaps.

Somehow, maybe because of his years of dealing with troubled kids, Riley sensed what was in Chaney's mind. He lunged toward the door and tried to open it, but the electronic system had disabled the door handles. "Stop that!'' Chaney ordered.

Riley turned back toward Chaney.

"People have to pay for the wrong things they do,'' Chaney said. "That's what you taught us, wasn't it? You'd get up at those assemblies, and we'd be sitting out there in our white shirts and red ties. And you'd give us those little lectures on social responsibility. Don't litter the halls. Don't drink alcohol. Don't drive fast. And if you did any of those things, you told us, you'd have to pay. Now tell me, if we had to pay, why shouldn't *you* pay?''

"Because I didn't do anything wrong."

"Really? Arrogant to the last, aren't you?"

"What are you going to do, Mark?" Riley asked.

Chaney wouldn't answer.

"What will you do, Mark? If they catch you, you know what'll happen? Where you'll go? It won't be a little institution this time, Mark."

"There you go," Mark said. "Another little lecture on social responsibility. You high-school principals never change, do you?"

Suddenly there was a lightning flash.

And Chaney waited for the thunder that would follow seconds later.

When it came, he squeezed slowly.

No one heard.

The plastic covers kept the seat from getting messy.

7

There were blankets in the trunk this time, so the ride back to New Rochelle was relatively quiet. Chaney felt a serenity, a contentment, born of a job well done and thoroughly relished. He was enjoying this project far more than his material success, which had already netted him close to a million dollars. That was financial security. This was revenge. No contest.

There was a special bonus because he'd been able to talk to Riley, even get in a few lines of the school anthem, which he now sang out loud to stay awake while driving. He knew that there were only four or five more of these nights before the project was completed, and he looked forward to each one.

The trip back up the New Jersey Turnpike was uneventful. The rain stopped, making driving easier. Chaney turned on the radio to hear Larry King interview a couple of investigative reporters, and he was interested enough in government scandals to listen. For a few minutes he almost forgot how important this night was, how exciting was the cargo in his trunk.

And then, as he approached New York, the monotony stopped. The uneventful became eventful. The sure thing turned into a maybe. Something was happening, something Chaney had never anticipated.

The New Jersey State police were conducting searches at tollbooths, looking for drugs. Chaney had read something about it in the paper, but it had never registered. He had read that some group was mounting a constitutional challenge, but he'd never given it a thought. Now he hated himself for being so indifferent, for letting standards slip, for not watching every detail, as a perfect killer should. There was always something out there ready to go wrong, wasn't there? There was always someone out there ready to grab Emil and him. He should have known. It was always the same.

Even now, in the middle of the night, there was a line of cars backed up a quarter mile, as every third car was checked thoroughly, its passengers frisked, its trunk and engine compartments opened. Sniffing dogs were everywhere, going over ever inch of idling vehicles, their engines chugging in the night. Chaney guessed it would take half an hour to get through this. But time was hardly his greatest worry.

If his number came up, he had to be prepared. But how could he, with the kind of package he had in his trunk?

Don't panic, he told himself.

No matter what happens, don't panic.

But he couldn't get out of the line. Cars trapped him on all sides.

He inched closer to the tollgate, smelling the fumes from the belching Buick ahead. He tried to stretch his neck to count cars, to see if he was among the chosen, but a Ford minivan blocked his view. He began to sweat. Even in the cool evening mist he switched on the air conditioner. Don't let the sweat show. Don't advertise concern. That was lesson one.

The cars moved ahead, starting then stopping, waiting for the inspections; drivers stuck their heads out the windows in anger and frustration. Finally, as the minivan went through the tollgate without being inspected, Chaney could count the cars ahead. Of course. He was a three. They'd be opening that trunk.

His mind raced. He saw a chance to squeeze out of line and head for another tollbooth, hoping his number wouldn't come up at that one. But it would draw attention, and he'd probably be searched simply because of the maneuver.

He could challenge the search on constitutional grounds, the way that group did, hoping to be let through as someone too troublesome to search. But he recalled reading that searches of this kind had been declared legal by some federal court.

He knew there was no way out. He kept moving ahead. Finally, with the two cars in front of him waved through, he came face to face with Sergeant Keenan Donald—according to the name tag above his pocket—a state trooper in brown uniform, wearing aviator glasses, his eyes rigid and focused. Donald, who looked to be in his forties, clearly had been picked for this duty because of his size: six feet three and almost as wide. Motorists were not encouraged to displease him.

"Sir, would you get out of your car," Donald ordered Chaney in an experienced voice that mixed courtesy with threat.

"Sure," Chaney answered. He got out of the car.

"Please stand next to the left front wheel," Donald then ordered. Chaney did what he was told.

Donald reached in, turned off the ignition and took the key. Then he began a thorough visual check of the passenger compartment and the underside of the dashboard. "Carrying any controlled substances?" he called to Chaney.

"No, of course not," Chaney replied. The air seemed colder to him now, and some late drizzle began coating his cheeks.

"Where you heading?" Donald asked, his voice muffled by the inside of the car.

"Westchester," Chaney replied. "I had business in Philadelphia."

Now Donald pulled the lever to release the hood. He went to the front of the car and snapped the hood up. Using his own flashlight, he began inspecting the engine compartment. "Ever been arrested?" he asked.

"No," Chaney lied, ignoring an impressive adolescent arrest record.

"Looks clean," Donald said, completing his sweep of the engine. He slammed the hood shut. Next he started walking around the car, flashing his light into the wheel wells, then placing himself on the ground, on a poncho, and inspecting the undercarriage, looking for hidden storage bins. He got up and returned to Chaney. "You're clear," he said. "New Jersey apologizes for the inconvenience, sir. We've got a gigantic drug problem. Really gigantic."

"Oh, I understand," Chaney said. "Look, this is important." My God, he thought, the guy forgot to check the trunk. Or maybe he'd been convinced by Chaney's appearance alone that he wasn't dealing with a drug trafficker.

Incredible. Miraculous.

Nonchalantly, Chaney walked back to the driver's door, opened it, and slid back into his seat.

He reached for the ignition key. It wasn't there. Donald had taken it. Chaney didn't have a duplicate. He had to get the key back from Donald. But would that remind him of what he'd missed? For a moment, Chaney just froze.

"You can go," Donald said.

Chaney didn't move.

"You can go, I said," Donald repeated, getting a little annoyed at the delay. "You got a problem, sir?"

"My key," Chaney said.

"Oh, right, I got it here," Donald laughed. As Chaney lowered his window, Donald handed the key to him. "Sorry," he said.

Chaney started the car. He reached for the transmission lever to put it back in "drive." And he began moving ahead. He went through the tollbooth, paid his toll, and started on, engulfed by a sense of overwhelming relief.

And then Donald realized.

He grabbed his whistle, hanging from a laniard.

"Stupid," he mumbled. "I forgot to check . . ."

But then he looked around. There were superior officers there. It would be embarrassing.

He let the whistle go.

Respectable men from Westchester didn't smuggle drugs anyway.

Anne had her leather-bound diary out. As a diary, it wasn't very intimate. She had a fear of dying suddenly, having the diary discovered by some lawyer or court officer, and read in places where it shouldn't be read. So Anne Seibert's diary was tame, revealing some feelings, but usually pulling its punches. One of the great gossip columnists of our time she was not. She made entries only intermittently, sometimes skipping days or even weeks, once skipping an entire summer. While waiting for Mark's return, periodically glancing out that living-room window, she jotted down a few thoughts:

"He's out again tonight. Wish I could get him to lead another kind of life. Maybe I can. Bradshaw thinks I'm on the right track. He's been right on everything else so far. I'll follow his advice. Very sleepy now, but I know can't sleep until Mark comes home. Shouldn't make judgments so soon, but he's old-fashioned terrific."

Anne wondered if *that* was a little too intimate for her proper diary but decided it could stay in. She wrote a bit more, then put the diary on a small table, next to her camera, and started reading a book about the German automobile industry. Required reading at Stellar Motors.

She looked out the window and saw a patrol car, just like the one that had passed Mark's house earlier in the evening. Again it stopped, and again the officers seemed to be observing the house. But Anne thought nothing of it. That's what police were supposed to do when a house was empty, and dark, especially if the owner had reported that he was going away.

It was 1:20 A.M.

Chaney entered New York State over the George Washington Bridge and started up the Henry Hudson Parkway, heading for Westchester County. But he diverted to Yonkers on his way up so he could stop and grab a late-night sandwich. He felt safe now, away from roadblocks and tollbooths, away from the well-patrolled superhighways. He was hungry and wanted to relax.

His Jaguar was equipped with a sophisticated antitheft system that made it virtually impossible for a thief to start the car, unless he wanted to spend about twenty minutes figuring out how the system worked. This eliminated one of Chaney's fears—that while he was away from the Jag, it would be stolen, along with its precious cargo. With the system installed he could sit down at an all-night luncheonette and feel relatively calm, knowing Riley would be there when he got back.

He ordered a bacon, lettuce, and tomato on white toast, with a side order of home fries and a chocolate shake. The meal was loaded with calories, but he felt he deserved to be rewarded after his brilliant night's work. He ate slowly, reading the first edition of *The New York Times*, which had just come in. Chaney turned to the business pages, reviewing the prices for mutual fund shares and leading stocks, making mental notes on the advice he would give clients the next day. He was careful not to let his and Emil's project interfere with business.

He finished, paid his bill, and left, cruising to the Cross County Expressway, and eventually into New Rochelle. As usual, he pulled into that closed service station to make his ritual call to Emil Welder, who, he knew, was waiting up to get the full story. Chaney got out of his car, went to the phone, and dialed.

The phone rang only once.

Welder picked it up. "Yes?" he asked urgently.

"It's Mark."

"Finished?"

"Of course. Everything was superb. Four-star. We even had a little conversation. He understood what he had to understand. You would have been pleased."

"Incredible," Welder said, his heavy breathing rushing through the phone line. "Were there any problems at all?"

"No. There was a drug roadblock when I came back, but nothing happened."

"You know what I can't wait to see?" Welder asked.

"No, what?" Mark answered.

"The alumni bulletin. They'll have to say something. I can see all the accolades. Maybe I'll write one myself." He laughed, and Mark could almost feel Emil's whole body shaking.

"Maybe we'll set up a scholarship in his honor," Mark countered. "Given to the best student convicted of a violent crime."

Again Welder laughed. "Only murder," he said. And they both laughed. It was a wonderful way to get rid of the tension.

"I'd better get out of here," Chaney said.

"Sleep well," Welder told him.

Chaney hung up and returned to his Jaguar. He drove the short distance to his neighborhood and turned down his street.

Was she there?

He drove slowly, hoping to study Anne's house as he pulled into his own driveway. But from halfway down the block he already had a hint of the answer. The living-room light was on, as it had been so many of those other nights. He drove farther, ready to turn into the driveway. He glanced toward Anne's window.

He saw her.

She was staring through the blinds.

It sickened him.

For a moment, he thought of acknowledging her, even waving, making it look as if he were glad to see her waiting up for him. But he decided against it, thinking it might seem a little too planned, a little too gracious. He pulled into his driveway, then swept around to the back of the house. He was excited at being home, bringing in the goods, but this *wasn't* perfect. True, Anne couldn't see the back of his house from her window, but the woman was *there*, shoving her face through those blinds, always watching.

* * *

Anne continued looking through the blinds, hoping for a glimpse of Mark as he walked through his house. She could hear him pull around to his back door, then cut his engine, then slam the car door after he got out. In the dead of night, the sounds traveled so easily.

She was sure she heard his back door squeak as he opened it.

But then—another part of his car opened and closed. It didn't have the solid sound of a door. From the muffled, hollow sound, Anne guessed it was the trunk. But she couldn't quite figure that. All right, maybe Mark had something in his trunk. But why did he open his house door first? Why wouldn't he have opened the trunk, gotten whatever it was, *then* gone to the house?

Then again, Anne thought, why did it matter?

Maybe he had something heavy. Maybe he'd bought something on the road. Stop wondering, she told herself. Stop worrying and letting everything consume you.

Now she heard Mark's house door slam. She knew what she wanted to do. She'd been thinking about it all evening.

She went to the phone.

Chaney almost buckled under Riley's weight. He approached the basement door carefully, his knees unsteady, trying not to fall. They seemed to be getting heavier and heavier each time, or was it that he was just getting older and more tired? He was almost there, starting to review the combinations to the two basement locks.

And then, two feet from the basement door, the phone rang.

Wrong number. No one called at that hour.

But no, maybe it wasn't a wrong number. Maybe it was Emil. Maybe he'd thought of something, or heard something on the radio about the disappearance of a retired principal.

Carefully, Chaney laid the cargo down, its green plastic wrap crackling with every move. He rushed to his living-room phone. "Hello?"

"Mark?"

"Anne! I knew I saw you up. More work?"

"Afraid so. They've really got me loaded. I guess you've been loaded too."

"Yeah, really weighed down. But I had a productive night."

"Great. But, look, you told me you liked hot cocoa and Premium crackers. I happen to have some hot cocoa and Premium crackers. How about it?"

Chaney just rolled his eyes. Hell of a time for a coffee break. "Sounds wonderful," he said. "Just let me get cleaned up and I'll jump right over."

"Ridiculous. I'll bring it over there."

"Anne, you don't have to come out in the night air. I wouldn't—"

"I'd love to," Anne replied. "You just relax. Give me about three minutes."

"Anne, you're wonderful. Why am I lucky enough to have someone like you living across the street?"

Anne loved that. Most men would just accept it, get what they could. This man had learned style from Cary Grant.

They hung up, and now Chaney did everything to control his rage. He couldn't have resisted her. She would have suspected something, correct? Probably. Or maybe he'd been paranoid. But paranoia was part of his makeup, and he wouldn't have it any other way.

He had only minutes to put Dr. Riley to bed. Hurriedly, he worked the combination on the first basement lock, unlatching it. He started on the second, his hands increasingly nervous as time elapsed. Two full turns left to 23, right to 41, left past 23 to . . .

What was it?

Was it 18? Or was it 8? It was 18. He turned to 18, then right to open.

But it didn't open. Was it 8? He tried the combination again. No results.

He'd forgotten that last number. Nerves, all nerves. With the clock ticking, he rushed to the desk in his bedroom. The combinations were stuffed in there somewhere.

As Mark opened the top drawer, Anne put everything she needed on a tray and started to leave her house. "Bye Freddie," she said to her Siamese cat, snapping off the living-room light.

Frantically, Chaney searched his desk, plowing through papers, mail, circulars, ads, and two worn copies of his high-school yearbook. He couldn't find that little yellow paper.

He rushed to his window.

There she was. Crossing the street. How long could he stall? How long could he hold her once she rang his bell? He ran back to the desk. He turned every drawer upside down.

And he found it.

The number was 12.

He darted back to the basement lock. Two full turns left to 23, then. . . .

The doorbell rang.

8
_

Chaney snapped the second lock.

He reached over to pick up the bulging green bag.

The doorbell rang again.

He didn't have time to walk Riley downstairs without revving Anne's suspicions. So he snapped the locks shut again. Looking around quickly, he decided to drag the body into a little-used bathroom near the kitchen. He deposited Riley in the bathtub and closed the curtain.

The doorbell rang a third time.

"Mark?" he heard her call out. Sure, she was one of those—the impatient type, the kind who wanted everything fast.

"Coming," he answered. He glanced in the bathroom mirror, saw that he was at least respectable, and went to the door. He urged a smile onto his fatigued face. "Anne, hello," he said, with a penetrating warmth, as if nothing had happened that night but a short ride to the corner drugstore.

She looked into those yearning, sizzling eyes, and the meltdown began. What a sight for an insomniac.

Anne swept in, fighting her own fatigue but trying to keep herself attractive. "I know this is crazy," she said, "but since we're both still up . . ."

"Who said it's crazy?" Chaney asked. "Here, let me take that tray. I'm just getting a second wind, and you're a lot prettier than the men I've been with all night."

"Hey, thanks," Anne said, walking on air into the living room as Mark placed her tray of goodies on a table. "You want to tell me about Albany before we chow down, or after?"

Jesus, Chaney thought, she was planning to stay. What was her motive? Did she see something when he came in? Did she hear something? Was she just testing to see if he could come up with something cogent about Albany? He had to play along. "Frankly, it wasn't all that exciting," he said. "I've got some clients up there who want to invest in biotech research, you know, gene-splicing and stuff like that. There's a company in California that's selling stock to expand. I gave my usual presentation, explaining the risks and rewards."

"There must be incredible risks," Anne said.

"Sure. If they do poor research, or someone beats them to a discovery, you're out of luck. If they hit right, you're a millionaire."

"Are they buying?"

Chaney sat down and stretched out, extending his hands behind his head and staring at the ceiling, pretending to relax. "Oh, I don't know," he replied. "These deep pockets don't make decisions quickly. They go over what I told them, then they consult with their partners and their lawyers and their lawyers and their lawyers. We're talking weeks or months."

"I still can't see why you drive," Anne said. "Wouldn't you be better off flying, or taking a train? You could sleep."

"But I couldn't make my own schedule. I love the independence. It's as simple as that."

"Besides, you have a Jaguar and you love *that*," Anne said.

"Guilty. For what they charge for that car, I want to live in it. Give you a ride some day."

"I'd love that," Anne said.

Mark had decided to be utterly charming. If she was suspicious, maybe it would deflect her, throw her off. Feelings always mattered, so why not turn his luck with women into a weapon?

"I'll get the snacks ready," Anne said. She took the tray and started into the kitchen. Mark got up to follow her. "Sit down," she said. "You've been driving all night."

"That's just it," Mark answered. "I've been sitting all that time. I like to move around."

Anne just smiled at him, frankly enjoying his company as she entered the kitchen. She began heating water for the cocoa and removed some Premiums from their green carton. "Like something on the crackers?" she asked.

"Margarine," Chaney replied. He went to the refrigerator and pulled out some Promise margarine, which, he'd heard, helped lower his blood cholesterol. He helped Anne spread the stuff on the crackers. "What kind of work you do yesterday?" he asked.

"I wrote a press release on a new fuel injection system. Mucho exciting. I have no idea what a fuel injection system is."

"It's more efficient than a carburetor," Chaney told her.

"Yeah, that's what one of the mechanics said. Frankly, it doesn't send me. Tomorrow I write some stuff on the new convertible they're bringing in. OK, that's got some zip to it.''

"Let me see what you write," Chaney told her. "I like convertibles. Maybe I'll buy one of yours."

"Really?"

"I'll give you the credit. Maybe they'll be generous."

"This company? Strictly by the ledger. There, I think the water's ready." She poured hot water into two cups, added the powdered cocoa, mixed it, and was ready to take everything into the living room. "Anything else?"

"No," Chaney answered. They both returned to the living room. Anne put the tray down on a low table.

"Yuch," Anne suddenly exclaimed. "I got some of that margarine on my hands. Off to the bathroom."

"Right next to my bedroom," Chaney said. "Just go down that hall—"

"Mark, didn't I just pass a bathroom?"

"Oh, yeah. There's one near the kitchen. Sure." He watched Anne stare at him quaintly, as if he'd done something eccentric. Did she intentionally stage that? She headed toward the bathroom near the kitchen. Did she *want* to use that one? Or was he imagining things?

He waited as she closed the door. He heard the water go on. Now he eyed a cabinet where he kept, behind some books, a .38-caliber pistol with a silencer attached.

Then, she suddenly came out. "Mark, do you know there's a bad smell in there?"

"Yeah. It's in the plumbing. I've got to call someone."

"You'd better. That kind of thing can spread to the whole house, and you'll never get it out."

"You're right, you're right. I've been slumming it. I'll call tomorrow."

Anne never looked behind the curtain, at the real source of the aroma. And so Chaney passed another crisis.

He and Anne spoke for about an hour. She felt right at home with him, their conversation covering the taxes in New Rochelle and the other communities they'd surveyed before they decided on this particular town. Anne was tempted to hint at her insomnia, to make a little joke about it, but restrained herself. Maybe he'd recoil, be turned off. Men were funny that way. Why jeopardize a budding relationship?

Even the word *relationship* felt strange to her as it tumbled over in her mind. She'd been to his house twice, he hadn't been to hers, they really hadn't "gone out," and yet she felt it *was* becoming a relationship. She tugged at herself to remain realistic. She knew how women fantasized at times like this. But . . . he liked her. *That* was obvious. He could have made all kinds of excuses not to see her, but hadn't.

"When are you going away?" he finally asked.

"About a week or so."

"Well, remember, I'm going to take your cat and watch your house."

"I remember. I keep telling him every day."

"What's his name?"

"Fred. I know it's not original, but he's a Fred. I knew it the first minute I saw him."

"I'll get to know Fred pretty well," Chaney said. "I'll set up a bed for him in my room."

"Oh, I wouldn't do that," Anne said. "He likes to scratch around at night. He'll keep you up. And he enjoys basements. He really does. Why don't we set something up downstairs before I leave. He'll be fine."

"That might be all right," Chaney said. "If it's not too damp down there." What was she getting at? Did she want to go downstairs again? Chaney again grew uneasy. Here she was, practically inviting herself over in the middle of

the night, and now she's talking about the basement. But
would someone working for the police act like that? Maybe
she would, just to appear eccentric enough so he *wouldn't*
suspect her.

But why even ask these questions? Why not just get rid of
her? Use the gun. Dump her body somewhere. She'd just be
another missing person. Sure, he'd be questioned by the
police since he's in the neighborhood. But he could cover it
well. They'd have no real reason to suspect him, and
certainly no evidence. Why continue to worry?

But was it rational? Was it the kind of thing the perfect
killer would do? Emil probably wouldn't approve of such
rash action, such gambling.

But he'd always taken risks, with or without Emil Welder. The wondering about Anne was getting to him. He knew
it could distort his already distorted mind. It could burn up
his energy, his attention, maybe even lead to a massive
blunder in his major project. The perfect killer could not
afford to be distracted.

He got up. He started walking to the cabinet where the
.38 was kept. He had his back to Anne, his body blocking
her view. But again he doubted. Was this right? Or was his
mind warped by fatigue?

"What are you getting?" she asked.

"Oh, just looking for something," he said. He took the
pistol from the cabinet, turned slightly, and slipped it into
his trouser pocket, so she still couldn't see. "You know, I'm
hungrier than I thought," he told her. "Walk me into the
kitchen. I'll grab a sandwich."

"Sure."

If he was going to do it, he had to do it in the kitchen. He
couldn't get the blood out of a living-room rug, but the
kitchen had one solid sheet of linoleum, highly waxed, and
that would be an easy clean-up. There were plenty of green

plastic bags in the pantry, and he could even keep her until the next day, then drive her to a desolate lot.

"Want me to make it for you?" she asked.

"That would be nice," Mark answered. "Why don't you just pull out some peanut butter and jelly."

She started to work. He stood back, in the center of the kitchen, his hand on the pistol in his pocket. Slowly, he reached in and released the safety lever. He began withdrawing the gun, just as she was slopping some peanut butter on a piece of low-calorie white bread.

The weapon was halfway out.

But . . . wait.

He eased it back in. There was one thing he hadn't thought of, one thing that made this a potentially ridiculous risk. What if she *was* working for the police, and what if she'd *called* her police contact and told him that she was going over to Mark Chaney's house and would check in again when she returned?

That decided it. If she didn't return, he'd be as good as convicted. He snapped the safety switch back on and took his hand from his pocket.

He tried to enjoy his sandwich.

He and Anne had their first "real" date set for Sunday. Mark had ideas, some very private ideas.

Later, he walked Anne back across the street. "I want to be sure you're safe," he told her.

9
—

Chaney finally got Dr. Riley into the deep freeze, replacing another guest, who'd been relocated. Then he watched from a darkened room as the lights in Anne's house went out one by one. And again, he was uneasy. Why did she suddenly turn the lights out? Presumably, she'd been working before he came home. Had her work suddenly ended with his arrival? Or was she simply too tired to stay up any longer? But, then, why had she come over if she was still working, and knew she wouldn't be able to finish after she returned?

She seemed responsible. That was not the behavior of a responsible person.

Too many things seemed to confirm Chaney's suspicions. He was anxious to see Anne again. He had to learn everything about her.

Chaney himself had a hard time sleeping. There was so much on his mind, so much to handle.

Anne slept well.

There was no better cure for insomnia than a few hours

with Mark, and a date to see him again. She dreamed about him, fantasized about him, worried about him.

She knew even before falling asleep that she'd never make it to work on time the next morning. She was simply too exhausted, and she felt she'd dipped into irresponsibility by visiting Mark in the middle of the night. She didn't regret it, really, but she did feel guilty. Her work was still her security blanket.

At 9:00 A.M., when her alarm rang, Anne reached over to her phone and dialed Stellar Motors.

Stellar's line rang only once.

"Carol Trager please," Anne said, when the receptionist answered. There were some clicks, and Anne heard another phone picked up.

"Carol Trager here."

"I'm a casualty," Anne said.

"Hey, Annie? What's wrong?"

"I stayed out a little late with himself last night, that's what's *right*."

"You takin' some time to sleep him off?"

"Yeah. I've got to. I'll take half a sick day."

Carol began to laugh. "I've seen it happen, kid, but not this fast. This guy's really got you."

"You may just be right."

"So when do you meet the family?"

"Oh, come on."

"No, I mean it."

But there was only silence from Anne. "Annie, you there?" Carol asked.

"I'm here," Anne said. "You know, it's funny. We talked the old blue streak last night, and he never mentioned his family."

"You gonna worry about it? Look, maybe his parents are, you know, permanently indisposed."

"Yeah. Maybe. If the right moment comes, I'll ask him."

"Annie, you go back to bed," Carol insisted. "I'll cover for you. And you sleep away the worries. You've got a budding deal there that half this country would kill for. Now dream about Mr. Right, and I'll see you later."

"Thanks, Carol. I'll make it up to you." Carol was always so amazingly reassuring, just the voice Anne always needed to hear.

She got off the phone just in time to hear Mark's Jaguar starting up across the street. She rushed out of bed and peeked out the window. She wanted to wave, but no, that would be too forward. Besides, it wasn't right that she was home. He'd think less of her. She cringed back into bed and pulled the covers up over her eyes.

Carol wasn't the only one thinking about Anne that morning. Mark Chaney kept wondering about the menace who lived across the street. And then there were the two men in the black Ford, parked down the block from Anne, who also thought about her, waiting for her to leave. They kept checking their watches, wondering why she wasn't coming out, curious as to why she'd broken her schedule. Maybe she was sick. Maybe she wasn't going to work at all. Maybe Mark had given her something to do at home. Maybe something had happened to her.

Right. Maybe something *had* happened to her. That's what you get for getting involved with Mark Chaney.

The two men sat slumped in the front seat, periodically jotting down the time and writing "no activity" on small pads that each kept in his lap. Detective Third Grade Seymour Castle, New Rochelle Police Department, and Sergeant Larry O'Grady, New Rochelle Police Department, didn't particularly care for surveillance duty. It was boring, rarely led to any great discoveries, and did little to advance their careers.

Castle was forty-two, a veteran of twenty years on the force, slim, with an unruly mustache that dominated his face and literally rippled in the breeze. O'Grady was twenty-nine, a former minor league baseball player who followed his father onto the force. He was a redhead who always wore aviator glasses and smoked miniature cigars. He thought the accessories helped his image.

"I'm gettin' worried," Castle said in his dull monotone. "Maybe one of our guys should ring her bell. Y'know, say he's a salesman."

"Maybe. Look, let's wait awhile," O'Grady said. "She was up late. Maybe she's out like a light."

"We sure she was with him?"

"Buck saw her go over, right in the middle of the night."

"Carrying a tray, I think he said," Castle recalled. "Transferring stuff. I wonder how she got involved."

O'Grady just shrugged, removed his sunglasses, breathed on them and cleaned them with his plainclothes sleeve.

"It's the money," Castle continued, answering his own question, his mustache bobbing. "What else could it be? I'll bet he's scamming her."

"Probably. My mother got caught in that kind of thing. Lost five hundred bucks. Now this girl, she just moved into the neighborhood. He probably saw her in the street and got her started. That's the way they work."

"Yeah," Castle said. "I know the type. He'll be gone in two weeks."

Then the two braced as they saw Anne's front door slowly open. "Well, what do you know," Castle said. "Still breathing."

They watched as Anne walked to her Oldsmobile, and

after five tries with the starter, got it going. She pulled out of her driveway and headed down the block.

"All right, let's go," Castle said.

O'Grady was driving; he started the Ford. They followed Anne at a distance, barely keeping her in sight. Because of jurisdictional rules, they could tail her only to the New Rochelle border. From there they watched as her Oldsmobile headed south, toward New York City. Both knew her link to Mark Chaney was continuing. What they didn't know, what their superiors *had* to know, was her precise relationship with her charming neighbor.

Chaney plunged into a business meeting with two wealthy investors from Toronto who were interested in getting into the electronics business. Dressed in an elegant gray suit, he sat next to Emil Welder, who, despite a reasonable effort in a blue blazer, always looked like he was going to burst out of his clothes. It had been a hectic morning, and Chaney hadn't even had a chance to speak privately to Emil. He couldn't wait but would have to now. He had to put on a good show for the investors. But his mind was on Anne Seibert.

The four men sat around a teak table in a room at M.E., Inc. A butler served coffee as they spoke, always keeping the cups filled almost to the top.

"I think it's a fine company," Chaney was telling the two dour-faced millionaires, neither of whom said a word. "They manufacture a new car radio that's three times more powerful than anything on the market. We see expanding possibilities for products like that."

"And their stock is cheap," Welder added, breathing heavily with each word. He was not an attractive figure at these meetings, but investors respected his intelligence.

"They have things in development," Chaney droned on.

"A car TV for the back seat that doubles as a computer terminal." Now he just couldn't wait any longer. He started writing little notes and passing them to Welder as he tried to sell the investors on his new corporate find. The investors thought he was simply jotting business ideas.

"She came over last night," Mark wrote, as Welder watched carefully. "Lots of questions. Don't think she's working late."

"You still seeing her Sunday?" Welder wrote back, as Chaney was explaining how the company was financed.

"Yes. Want her to be seen in certain places—the kind where people go to end it all."

"Good. I have suggestions," Welder wrote.

"Something else," Mark said in his next note. "Today. Pulling out. Saw parked car. Certain I recognized driver as cop. Once saw him at headquarters when I reported lost watch."

"Think *she's* involved in that?" Welder wrote.

"Don't know. Cop may not even be for me. Just one more thing to worry about. But she's got nothing on me. Everything's hidden."

Chaney cleared his throat. "So you see, gentlemen," he went on, "—and I know from these notations that we're jotting that Mr. Welder agrees with me—I would move your investments out of chemicals into this firm. It's a good bet. Not sure. It never is. But good."

Welder kept writing. "You ready for Miss Burnette?" he wrote to Chaney.

"Sure. About a week," Chaney wrote back. "She's returned to Washington, D.C. Long night trip, but I'll do it."

"I hated her. She talked down to us," Welder wrote, his writing suddenly dissolving into a scrawl when he thought back to Miss Burnette.

"They all talked down to us," Chaney wrote on his little

pad, while explaining to his clients that a three-million-dollar investment would be the minimum acceptable to the firm involved.

The investors then asked a small number of questions, and the meeting ended, with neither of them giving any commitments. Ironically, Chaney and Welder had little new to talk about, having made all the relevant points in their notes. They returned to their offices, where Chaney began planning his first real date with Anne. Depending on how things went, it could also be their last.

Chaney had asked his secretary to get him travel folders about the New York area, ostensibly for a client who wanted to take his children to the city. Actually, he used them to do some preliminary research. He'd concluded that if he had to kill Anne and disguise her death as a suicide, a jump from a high point would be the easiest method to arrange, just as he'd originally proposed to Emil. The folders, with their exotic views of the region, often photographed from heights, gave a pretty good indication of some of the more unusual spots that were available. Mark quickly noted a few that felt right: small bridges that might be deserted, buildings with windows that weren't sealed, cliffs along the Hudson River. He particularly liked the cliffs, for they were often shielded from view by shrubs and trees.

He checked the driving distance to each potential location, hoping to find one that wouldn't require a long, tortuous drive through thick traffic. A long, unpleasant drive could make a potential victim suspicious, and put her on guard.

Research, Chaney had always said to his firm's employees, eliminates 90 percent of problems before they arise.

He always practiced what he preached.

* * *

Chaney went into Welder's office an hour later, finding Welder at his desk reading a copy of a newspaper and beaming broadly, his many chins stretched to their limit. "What is it?" Chaney asked, closing the door behind him.

"I love this rag," Welder replied. "It's the perfect newspaper for our kind of thing." He flipped the paper on the desk so Chaney could see it. There, splashed on page three, was a picture of Dr. Riley as he'd appeared years before, when he was a Long Island high-school principal. The headline, over a full-page story, read "BELOVED PRINCIPAL MISSING."

"Beloved," Chaney mumbled. "Warm, kindly Dr. Riley. So beloved."

"The morons loved him," Welder replied, bursting out in a laugh that fairly shook the room. "They called him Mr. R and smiled at him when he walked down the hall. People like Riley, they always get someone to love them."

Chaney started reading the story:

> "A former high-school principal from the metro-politan area, beloved by his students and faculty, was reported missing last night by police in Phila-delphia, where he'd lived since his retirement. His abandoned car was found only blocks from his home.
>
> "The educator, Dr. . . ."

"We pulled it off," Chaney said, always using "we" to make sure Welder felt part of the action. "The police can look all they want. They'll never get outside Philadelphia."

"I wonder if we'll be able to kill all of them," Welder replied. "We've been lucky. If there's a God, he's been with us."

"He'll stay with us, Emil," Chaney said. "He knows

where evil is. We'll get them all. I won't make any mistakes. God protects those who are perfect.''

"I believe that,'' Welder answered, glancing down at the paper and smiling again. "Watch,'' he said. "Next edition they'll have a picture of Riley's closest relative holding a picture of him.''

"And he'll say that his dear old uncle wouldn't hurt a fly,'' Chaney added. "The most decent man you could think of. Probably out picking up the homeless.''

"You working on Burnette?'' Welder asked.

"No. Right now I'm working on Sunday. That's when I see this snooping woman. Emil, there's no doubt we have a problem. Too many things are coming together. And those cops on the block this morning.''

"But you said they could've been for someone else.''

"Yeah, but what are the odds?'' He paused, wondering whether to bring up the next subject. But he'd always been straight with Welder, and he would be straight now. "I almost killed her last night.''

"You almost what?''

"Killed her, Emil. With a pistol. But I thought it was rash.''

"I should say so. Look, Mark, don't let her get to you like that.''

"I'm not. It was a weak moment. But she's a distraction. She's draining my energy and time. By the way, I *am* taking her to the Jersey Palisades on Sunday, exactly as we'd discussed. That's the right spot.''

"You've decided to *do* it?''

"No. Not really. I keep thinking it over. I change my mind. Plans should always evolve. The way I look at it, there's really no point in doing it now... unless it becomes absolutely necessary. She's up to something, but I don't know exactly what or who she works for. She acts crazy, bringing me stuff in the middle of the night. I can't quite figure this. She's either a brilliant operator or a complete blunderer.

"No, I still want to learn about her. The more I know about her, and what she really wants, the more I can learn about the people behind her... if there are any."

"Why the Palisades?" Welder asked.

"I want to go there a few times with her. Let her mention where we go to her friends. Let her be seen there, even with me. If it comes to it, it would be the logical place for a jump. People would say, 'She went there all the time. She liked it. She was planning it all along. She had divorce problems.' You agree?"

"Mark," Emil said, "when it comes to killing, I always agree with you."

They spoke in their cool, almost detached way, yet each man knew that the cloud over them wasn't getting any thinner. Anne *was* distracting them, yet they knew she could be more than a distraction. She might be their undoing.

If only they could know the truth.

If only they could safely get her out of the way.

10

Sunday was a warm and balmy day, perfect for an outdoor excursion, perfect for Mark Chaney to take Anne Seibert on a tour of possible death sites.

Anne was excited as she primped before the bedroom mirror, the slightly open blinds allowing her to glance over at Mark's house. She wondered what guardian angel had made her move across the street from Mark Chaney, that superb and gentle man.

Actually, her weekend had been rushed. She was getting ready for her Tuesday trip to Detroit, catching up on press releases she hadn't written, and doing some preliminary packing. But Mark was the highlight. She looked forward to the conversation, to learning more about him, to feeling part of his life.

The recurrent fear of making another mistake, a repeat of her first husband, was always there. Yet, she knew there was one mistake she *couldn't* make. Her first husband had shown some violent tendencies from the first moment she'd met him, but when he blew up at a waiter and pushed a garage attendant she'd chosen to look the other way. Nerves, she'd rationalized. Mark was clearly the opposite. He had his head on straight. There wasn't a violent bone in his body. She felt so safe with him.

She heard him honk a few minutes later, just as they'd arranged. She waited a few minutes more—the usual respectable delay—then started out. Wearing a pink dress and a white, open sweater, she left her house, feeling like a teenage girl, and piled into Mark's Jaguar.

"You're right on time," she said, hating the usual small talk at the beginning of these dates.

"I'm used to schedules," Mark replied.

It was the first time Anne had seen him in informal clothes: khakis, a sport shirt, and a leather jacket. With his slim physique the guy could be a model, she thought.

"Great car," she said. "Even though I work for the competition."

"I hadn't thought of that," Mark laughed. "Well, you'll have to demonstrate one of those hot rods you're importing. As I said, I just may switch."

Mark moved quickly through New Rochelle, negotiating around Sunday drivers and occasional bicyclists, and headed for the major roads.

"I'm glad we're going to the Palisades," Anne said. "I've never been up there. I mean, I've passed in a car, and I once went to Palisades Amusement Park when it was open, but I've never walked there."

"Great area," Mark replied. "The view of the Hudson is spectacular. I used to go there when I was in high school."

"Oh. You come from this area? I didn't know."

"Bell Grove, on eastern Long Island," Mark said, just as they were spinning onto the Bronx River Parkway for the trip south.

"Bell Grove," Anne said. "That's familiar."

"Small town," Mark told her. "A lot of people from Grumman, the plane company."

"Bell Grove," Anne repeated. Then she turned to him, an eery expression on her face. "Mark, did you go to high school there?"

"Yeah."

"And you're not . . . upset?"

"Upset?"

"Wasn't that principal who disappeared in Philadelphia from Bell Grove?"

Mark glanced over at her. She'd maneuvered the conversation so well. It was another nail in her coffin. "Yeah, he was," he replied. "He was *my* principal. And, yeah, I'm upset. But I mean, it was years ago. I really don't think about that time very much. Still, I was pretty shocked to hear what happened."

"Did you ever talk to him?"

"Dr. Riley? Sure. I liked him. He had a good sense of humor. It's a horrible thing. Sometimes I guess we don't feel it that much for people that old. Frankly, I was surprised he was still alive. But whoever did that, they oughta put him away."

"Or shoot him," Anne said.

"No. I'm against capital punishment," Mark answered. "No one has a right to take a life. Put him away forever."

Anne was warmed by the answer. Despite her bravado, she'd always been against capital punishment too, unlike her first husband, who favored firing squads. Mark's comment made her respect him even more. "Right. Put him away," she said. But then something else popped into her mind. "Mark," she asked, "why do you assume someone did something?"

"What?"

"To that principal. The paper just said he was missing,

disappeared off the face of the earth. They didn't find any blood, or any sign of foul play. Why did you assume . . . ?''

"How else could he be missing?'' Mark broke in, playing a kind of dumb he didn't like to play but feeling it necessary.

"Maybe he just decided to go away,'' Anne said. "I read that most people listed as missing persons *want* to be missing.''

"You had to know this guy,'' Mark answered. "He wasn't that type. Also, why park your car a couple of blocks from your house? If a guy wants to go away, he can just drive to a train station and go.''

"You're probably right,'' Anne said.

"One of my clients once disappeared,'' Mark continued, in a thorough lie. "He was one of the ones who wanted to go, to get rid of all his problems. But he took a wad out of the bank first. There was nothing in the paper about Dr. Riley doing anything like that. I think it was a robbery that went bad. I hate that kind of thing. Fine old man like that.''

They both fell silent for a time, Anne realizing she'd been a fool to bring up the subject. It put Mark into the kind of mood she didn't want. She was always doing that, she thought, always opening her mouth and letting the wrong words come out.

Now she wanted to talk only of happy things.

They arrived at a quiet place near the Jersey Palisades, just north of the George Washington Bridge. It had not yet been pillaged by developers. They parked near some other cars and prepared to get out of the Jaguar. But first Mark reached into a leather case he kept in the back seat and pulled out a Polaroid camera, bringing it forward and draping the strap over his shoulder.

"You brought your camera,'' Anne exclaimed. "That's

terrific." It was another sign, she was sure, of his interest in her.

"Well, I like mementos," Mark said.

And of course he did want mementos, visual reminders of the area to study later if he decided to go through with Anne's "suicide." He'd used the Polaroid often in his and Emil's project, taking pictures of all the places where he intended to meet his victims. He had more than ten Polaroids of Dr. Riley's car, which he kept in an album in a safe. Occasionally he and Emil went through the album almost the way parents would review pictures of their infant children.

Anne and Mark started walking toward the cliffs. There were plenty of other people out, and an army of vendors was selling ice cream, newspapers, and film. Mark edged Anne away from a newspaper vendor when he glanced at a front page and saw a story about Dr. Riley. Let's have no more talk about that.

"You do a lot of photography?" Anne asked him.

"No, not really. I have this and a 35-millimeter camera. But I'm a three-roll-a-year man. I guess if I were married, with kids, I'd do a lot more."

"I bet you would," Anne smiled, wondering if the first hint had just been delivered.

"You take pictures?" Mark asked.

"Rarely. I have a camera, but it stays inside most of the time. It was a gift. Oh, look at that view!"

They stepped to a position near a cliff and gazed out at the skyline of New York City through the cables of the George Washington Bridge.

"I'm glad we have a clear day," Mark said. "See the Statue of Liberty?"

"Sure. Of course, being a New Yorker, I've never been there."

"Neither have I. Well, we've got another trip, I guess."

"You guess right," Anne told him.

"Stand a little to your left," Chaney said. "Let me get a picture."

"You sure you want *me* in it?"

"Come on!"

Anne gladly obliged, awed at how perfectly everything was going. She could not know that Mark's motive was to flatter her at first, keep her happy, then snap some pictures *without* her, the pictures he had actually come to get.

He took his picture of Anne, then another with a different pose. But his eyes were everywhere. The nearest cliff had a drop of about two hundred feet, with rocks below. That would certainly do. But Mark wondered whether the area was too open, whether he could, even with great care, guarantee that no one would see him push Anne over the side. He snapped several pictures of the area, each time telling Anne that some unusual formation of trees or rock was catching his attention.

They walked a little farther, once again coming to a steep cliff. This one was more secluded, more to Mark's liking. He'd developed a practiced eye for locations, for the right place to perform the right act. It was part of the experience he'd gathered on his and Emil's project. He took a few obligatory pictures of Anne, then photographed the cliff.

"You're going to have a whole album of this place," Anne said, amazed at the speed with which Chaney was burning up film.

"I go a little crazy," Mark admitted. "I still get a kick out of watching the picture pop out of the camera and develop."

"A little crazy," Anne thought. If only he knew what crazy was. *She* knew, having lived with a crazy man, a man with violence deep inside him. She doubted that Mark Chaney had any idea what "crazy" actually meant. In fact, he seemed so boyish, snapping away with his Polaroid, taking pictures of little bits of scenery that really weren't very scenic. Boys need their toys, she'd always known. And this boy was no different.

"Watch out!" she suddenly shouted, as Mark walked close to the fence atop the cliff.

A fence post was bent, possibly loose.

"Thanks," he replied, veering away from the fence, now seeing what she'd seen.

He walked over and tested the post. Yes, it was very loose, and had he leaned against it he could have gone through. "Jesus," he said, "I could've been killed. Anne, I think you saved my life."

He rushed over to her and kissed her.

"I'm glad I noticed," she said quietly, shaken for a few moments, yet realizing that the near miss, the near tragedy, would form a further bond between them. "Please be careful, Mark."

"I will, I will."

Chaney reached into his pocket and pulled out a notepad, penning a warning note to other strollers and sticking it on the post. "I hope they fix this fast," he said. "I'll call the parks department. This is terrible."

But it was a wonderful spot, he told himself. In the time he and Anne had been there, no one else had come by. And the area at the bottom of the cliff was filled with brush. A body could lie there for a good long time without being discovered.

He turned back to Anne. She seemed to be deep in thought. "Something wrong?" he asked, as they started walking.

"I was just thinking," Anne answered. "You're so different from my husband. Just the way you thought to put that note on the post. He would've spun into a rage and pulled it right out of the ground.''

''That bad, aye?''

''Oh, he was bad.''

''Well, I try to stay in control,'' Chaney said. ''In my business, with all the stress, you've got to have some kind of system. And the first lesson in staying in control is . . . never take anything personally.''

''I don't know if I could do that.''

''Oh, you could do it. People are mostly decent. They usually don't mean to hurt you. The worst thing is to go through life bearing grudges. If you don't like someone, just go on, and try to smile.''

''You never bear a grudge?'' Anne asked.

''No. Never.''

She believed him. He was that kind of guy.

They drove home slowly, stopping at a Westchester shopping center where Chaney knew a great Chinese restaurant. After dinner—shrimp and chicken dishes—they dropped into the supermarket a few doors down to stock up, Anne suddenly feeling very, very domestic. Then they went back to Anne's house, where she rustled up some coffee and crackers.

It was at Anne's house that Chaney finally met Fred, Anne's large, black-and-white Siamese cat who would be his ward during the time she planned to be in Detroit. He asked all the right questions about Fred's care: the name of the veterinarian, danger signs, and what he could and couldn't eat. He forced himself to show concern for the cat, although he'd never liked animals and was convinced that some of them made him sneeze.

Besides, Dr. Riley had a cat when Chaney was in high

school. Fred brought back that memory. He hated the memory. He didn't feel too good about Fred.

"Uh, anything I should know about your house before you go away?" he asked Anne.

"Like what?"

"Well, like whether you're expecting any deliveries. I'll take them to my house if I'm still home in the morning."

"No, I don't think I ordered anything," Anne said.

"You should have an answering machine," Mark suggested.

"I do. By the way, would you like a key? In case of a problem you'd want to get in."

"No, I'd feel funny about having your key. Why don't you just leave me the name of your landlord. If anything's suspicious, I'll call him."

"Thanks," Anne said. "That's a relief."

"You told me before you didn't have a burglar alarm. Still?"

"Yes. Maybe I'll get around to it."

"Well, just make sure you have good locks."

"That I have. The Morgan locks. You know, dead bolt."

"Sure," Chaney said. "In the back too?"

"Yes. Both doors."

It was wonderful chatter, and Chaney was surprised that Anne was so giving. She had, after all, told him everything he wanted to know.

He was sure her trip was nothing more than a cover, a device to make her look thoroughly legitimate. But he was ready to turn it into something else, and Fred was going to help him. "Here Fred," he called out, as the cat crossed the living room. "I consider him a friend already," he told Anne.

He was the best kind of friend—the kind who couldn't talk.

11

Anne took off from Kennedy airport that Tuesday morning on a United flight to Detroit. Carol sat next to her aboard the 727, her hands shaking, her face bleached white, a prayer to each and every God on her well-lipsticked lips. Anne was exhausted from an insomnia-laden night, but could get no rest now. Her time was spent keeping Carol calm and trying to explain to her the positive statistics on aviation safety.

Even in the air, even with Carol's mental state, Anne missed Mark. She'd dropped Fred off that morning and knew he was in good hands. But she wished she were back in New York with the man across the street. He was becoming her life, the only thing she really cared about. They hadn't agreed to speak by phone during her trip—unless there were an emergency with Fred—but Anne now decided to place a phone call to Mark late that night. He said he'd be home sometime after eleven. Maybe a phone call would relax him.

The flight was uneventful, and despite Carol's trauma, it

seemed to pass quickly. Anne was finally able to get some work done, while still holding Carol's hand, and felt ready for the hectic days ahead.

Then, arrival.

"Ladies and gentlemen, we're about to land at Detroit, Michigan, the motor city," droned the flight attendant, getting a laugh from the Stellar Motors contingent aboard. Detroit to them was the enemy, the threat to their golden imports. After the laugh they all clipped on their seat belts and prepared to land, to invade the homeland of the automaker's Big Three.

Chaney didn't go to work that day. He had too much planning to do, too many tools to prepare. He did go out briefly to pick up *The New York Times*, which had been dropped near his bushes by the delivery boy, and noticed that the same two cops he'd seen before were down the block again. It was annoying, but he still had no direct evidence that they were there because of him. And he was *sure* they didn't know about his remarkable basement collection. If they'd known he was a multiple murderer, and that he could kill again, they surely would have moved in to prevent another death.

He had a full selection of pictures to study, taken discreetly over a period of days. One set showed his own neighborhood, particularly the houses surrounding Anne's house. Chaney wanted to know whether Anne's back door could be seen from any of those houses, and he concluded that it could. It was an additional risk for him to consider.

He also had a variety of Morgan locks that he'd bought at different hardware stores the day before. He practiced on each one, perfecting techniques he'd learned as part of his and Emil's project. It would have been easier had he known precisely which model Anne had on her back door, but he wasn't able to maneuver to that door when he was visiting.

One thing bothered him—Fred. Fred was a relatively quiet cat, but he kept going to the basement door and scratching. Obviously, his delicate nose detected something in the basement, a scent that would tantalize an animal. By mid-afternoon Fred had scratched some of the paint off the door, and Chaney finally decided to stow him in a bedroom. He made a note to repaint the door quickly.

Although Fred bothered him, as anything involving Anne would bother him, he knew the cat was critical to his plans.

Chaney scraped some of the gunpowder from inside a pistol and let Fred smell it. He then mixed it with some of Fred's food. He did this about fifteen times, giving Fred the idea that the smell of gunpowder would lead him to food. Chaney had no idea whether this would actually work, but he always prided himself on innovation.

He picked out a pair of rubber surgical gloves, making sure they were free of rips. He also checked all buttons on the clothing he would wear that night to see that they were secure. And he removed every superfluous item from his pockets. Nothing, Chaney knew, could ever be left to chance.

He recalled how a dropped pair of glasses led to the arrest of Leopold and Loeb. It had been a stupid blunder, the ruination of the perfect crime. But Mark Chaney would drop nothing.

Once he finished his preparations, he lay down and took a nap, putting everything out of his mind. He looked forward to the night. Mark Chaney always looked forward to the night, for that was when the only important work of his life was done.

As night fell in Detroit, Anne was getting ready for a party thrown by Stellar Motors. Most of the Detroit auto press would be there, as well as a group of race-car drivers flown in to add credibility to Stellar's performance claims. Anne's job would be to answer press questions about the cars' features. She'd been assigned a post next to one of the red, two-door models, which would be parked right in the center of the hotel ballroom.

She shared a room with Carol, Stellar being too cheap to spring for singles. Carol was past her flight nervousness, having replaced it with preparty nervousness. Both she and Anne primped in front of a mirror, each in the formal gowns the event called for. Carol tried to memorize some material on a fact sheet Stellar had given her. Anne's mind was hundreds of miles away.

"I wonder what he's doing now," Anne said.

"Hey, look, stop wondering," Carol answered. "He's probably with some filthy-rich client, conning him into buying some stock."

"He's not a con man."

"Sorry. You're right. Keep his image clean. Anywhere you can call him?"

"Not this early. He's out."

"Who feeds your tiger?"

"Fred? I fed him this morning. Mark'll give him a late-night snack when he gets in." She glanced at her watch. "It's eight o'clock. I'd better call my machine."

"Never call a machine early in the evening, honey. Friends call at night, and you won't pick 'em up for twenty-four hours. After the party, call."

"Yeah, you're right," Anne said.

In the background, they could hear the noise of guests rushing through the halls, trying to find the ballroom. Anne had been to many of these promotionals and hated one more than the other. The forced smiles. The hype. The hangers-on who came just for the food. When she contrasted the glitter with the homey atmosphere in New Rochelle, it just made her miss Mark even more.

She had this vision of him in his Jaguar, haggard after a day's work, preparing to take some dull executive out to dinner. She hoped he was thinking of her, thinking of how soon they'd be together again. She convinced herself that he was, that she was becoming as important to him as he was becoming to her. She began to think of gifts, even trinkets, that she might bring him from Detroit.

Chaney rested in bed, staring at the ceiling, thinking of Anne. How he hated women who tried to deceive him, as most of them did. How he wished something would happen to her on that trip to Detroit, so he wouldn't have to take more risks with her. Of course, in the back of his mind he still wondered if she might simply be a curious girl. But he really couldn't believe that, and he was eager for the hours to pass so he could edge closer to the truth and possibly clinch it.

He could not get that vision of her out of his mind—that vision of her at the window, watching him, studying him, spying on him. It was the only vision of her he ever had, the only way he could possibly remember her.

He loathed every moment with her, but every moment was necessary for his own protection.

He swung out of bed and breathed deeply to clear his brain. As Anne Seibert demonstrated the windshield wipers on a new FSR in Detroit, Mark Chaney glanced through his blinds at her house. She'd left a few lights on for security, and her battered Olds was parked in the driveway.

He had all his steps memorized. Anne had accommodated him by leaving Fred's travel box. He walked to his kitchen to grab a sandwich and prepare. He would wait until the lights in the neighborhood were off, until Anne's neighbors were asleep.

Then he would move.

In both Detroit and New Rochelle, the time passed slowly. The crowds lingered at the Stellar Motors party, the lingering in direct proportion to the amount of food brought into the crystal-chandeliered ballroom. The band was on overtime, playing soft music to preserve the ears of the guests and allow the sales pitches to flow. Anne was sitting on the sidelines now, trying to get some rest between aimless conversations with car dealers and race drivers. It was approaching ten o'clock in Detroit, eleven in New Rochelle. Soon she would be able to call. Tired though she was, she hoped she and Mark could talk an hour.

The neighborhood was quiet.

The car with the two cops was gone.

Mark Chaney snapped off his front light so no one would see him leaving and silently opened his front door. He carried a small bag of tools in one hand and Fred, in the traveling box, in the other. Clipped to his belt was a cordless telephone with a 1,000-foot range. Swiftly, watching for any sign of life, he slipped across the street to Anne's house, ducking behind her car for cover, listening for any sound that might indicate he was not alone. He heard nothing but the rustling of trees, and an occasional bird discouraged by a shortage of food.

He moved along a hedge line to the rear of the house. Fred let out a meow, but Chaney assumed, correctly, that neighbors were used to hearing cat sounds in the night. Anne's back door was on a terrace, which Chaney climbed next. Near the door was a security light. Chaney, wearing the surgical gloves to avoid leaving fingerprints, opened the little fixture and loosened the bulb, throwing the back of the house into darkness.

He looked around. Nothing was moving in the nearby houses. Working people went to bed early.

He set Fred's travel box on the terrace and started to work on the lock. It took him only a few minutes before the lock clicked open. Slowly, Chaney turned the knob, only a few millimeters at a time. He knew that any squeak or rattle now could alert half-awake neighbors. When he'd turned as far as he could, he gently pushed the door open.

It opened about two inches.

And stopped.

Anne hadn't mentioned, and Chaney didn't know, that she also had a chain on that door. When she'd left for Detroit, she'd gone out the front door, leaving the chain intact in the rear.

Chaney silently cursed himself. Why hadn't he noticed that chain the first time he'd snooped around Anne's house? Why hadn't he found a way to examine the rear door when he'd visited?

Dumb.

Inexcusable, like all mistakes.

Getting through the chain itself was no problem, Chaney knew. That he could simply cut. But then he'd have to buy another chain and return the next night to replace Anne's, so she wouldn't know there'd been a break-in. That magnified his risk, but now he had no choice. He studied the chain carefully in the light of a quarter moon, hoping it was the common type, not some designer special that would be hard to duplicate. He saw quickly that it was standard.

Chaney took a jeweler's saw from his little bag and started cutting through the chain. The metal was soft and cheap—any thief could get through it fast—and faded before the saw in less than two minutes. Now Chaney could open the door and get inside. He reached out, grabbed Fred's travel box and pulled him in too. He was about to close the door when . . . his cordless telephone began to ring.

He knew precisely who it was. He had the cordless phone with him to take her call in case he had to stay at her house longer than he'd anticipated. He knew she might become suspicious if she called very late and found him away.

But it wasn't *that* late, and he had too much to do. He decided not to take the call.

He knew she'd try again.

Anne was stuffed inside a hot phone booth, one of a row of six, just off the ballroom floor. Two half-sober auto executives waited impatiently outside, hoping for a phone to be free so they could call home and assure their wives that they were safe and loyal. Each executive had a date waiting in a car.

Finally, after eight rings, Anne decided to give up. She reluctantly returned the receiver, picked up her telephone charge card, and went back to the remnants of the Stellar Motors promotional party.

"Not home," she told Carol, who was entertaining an advertising executive who'd just gotten a divorce and was therefore interesting.

"It's early," Carol replied. "Now look, you're not gonna worry about that, are you?"

"He said he'd be home."

"Maybe he got a flat tire."

"Or another woman."

Carol rolled her eyes, well coated with mascara. "Or maybe a space ship landed in New Rochelle and took him to Mars."

"Carol, you're gonna give me something else to worry about," Anne said.

"Honey, I don't have to give you anything. You'll drive *yourself* nuts."

"It's a good form of nuts," Anne answered softly. She eyed the phone booths, which were filled, and started drifting toward them. She decided to try again in fifteen minutes. She pictured Mark returning to New Rochelle, anticipating her call, storing up things to tell her.

Mark was helped by the fact that Anne had left those few lights on. He couldn't, of course, turn on any more—any neighbor who was awake might see the light go on—but he carried a tiny flashlight with a dark red lens to use in darkened rooms.

He also had a Mini-Vac, a tiny, battery-powered vacuum cleaner that could not be heard beyond the house walls. He quickly used it to vacuum up the metal dust from his cutting the door chain. That finished, he was ready to do what he'd come to do.

His hands still gloved, Chaney crawled to the telephone Anne had in her kitchen. He crawled in order to avoid creating a silhouette in the window.

When he reached the phone he dialed Emil's number. He couldn't call Emil on his cordless phone because cordless transmissions were easily intercepted by anyone nearby who had a phone on the same frequency.

Emil picked up after one ring.

"Yes?"

"It's Mark. I'm inside."

"Problems?"

"One problem. I had to cut through a door chain. I'll have to come back and replace it."

"Is there time?"

"Yes. Tomorrow night. She won't be back."

"Good. You ready to work?"

"Ready."

They'd agreed that Chaney would report to Emil, by phone, anything suspicious that he found. This made it unnecessary for Chaney to spend time taking notes.

"I'll be right back," Chaney said. He placed the receiver down and started searching the kitchen first.

And the first thing he spotted was Anne's 35-mm camera.

Anne squeezed back into a booth. The fifteen minutes were still not up, but she wanted to be sure she had access to a phone. Besides, there was another call she wanted to make. She tapped in her telephone charge number and started dialing, calling her own number to check her answering machine.

She heard the usual clicks and buzzes as the phone equipment made the long-distance connection. And then there were a few seconds of silence.

And then there was a busy signal.

She couldn't understand it. How could there be a busy signal in an empty house?

Maybe she'd dialed a wrong number. She made a note to claim credit with the phone company and dialed again.

And again there was a busy signal.

Had she left the phone off the hook? No. She'd checked the phones before leaving home. Could the phone be out of order? That was a possibility, although she'd never had phone trouble.

Then it hit her. What if someone was calling and leaving a message on her machine? Of course. That would create the busy signal. And that someone could easily be Mark. Maybe he had to be late and decided to call the machine, hoping she'd check for messages. Anne began convincing

herself that this was the case. It was the story she wanted to
believe.

He was thinking of her, considerate of her. She was sure
of that.

"It's a Nikon," Chaney told Emil, "with a telephoto
zoom. Same camera I saw through the window."

"Is it loaded?" Welder asked, his breath rushing through
the phone lines.

Chaney checked the frame counter. "Yes, it's on number
14."

"Unload it. You know I've got a darkroom. I can develop
the film tonight. When you go back to replace that door
chain, you can put in a new roll and wind to number 14."

"Great idea, Emil," Chaney said, "but the new film'll
be blank."

"Mess up the camera a little," Welder said. "She'll think
it malfunctioned."

Chaney liked that. He and Emil had always worked so
well together. He opened the camera, unloaded it, and
slipped the roll of Kodak Tri-X film into his pocket. Then
he was ready for more work.

He crawled from room to room but was disappointed to
find nothing of great value. He heard Fred meowing in the
kitchen, reminding him that the cat would be performing a
mission of his own later on. Finally, Chaney crawled into
Anne's bedroom and, helped by his tiny flashlight, started
searching through her drawers, finding mostly notes from
her work, shopping lists, and some letters from friends.

But then he found something else.

He picked up the extension phone next to her bed.
"Emil," he reported, "there's a notepad here with the
names and numbers of New Rochelle cops. There's also a
business card from a private detective."

"Most people don't keep stuff like that," Emil said.

"No, they don't. Emil, it looks like someone after us again. These may be her contacts. The private eye might be doing some free-lance work . . . for her."

"They're garbage," Emil said.

Neither man dreamed that the police officers and private eye were listed as a precaution in case Anne had problems with her violent, former husband, who'd once made a threatening call to her. She'd never even met the people on that list. She never really wanted to.

Anne called her phone again, but the number was still busy. It was either a long message, she reasoned, or something *was* wrong with that phone. She thought of calling the operator to check, but a very angry reporter was waiting for her phone, so she decided to relinquish it. She was exhausted. She decided to go back to her room and try her calls from there.

Mark searched the rest of Anne's house, finding nothing of interest. He read some letters to a relative in Chicago, but they were months old and didn't mention him. He found Anne's date book, which noted their date on the Palisades. The rest was devoted to business.

Mark never found Anne's diary. She had it with her in Detroit.

After completing his basic search, he was ready for Fred, and for an exotic experiment. He let Fred out of his carrying box and started taking him around from room to room. He hoped that Fred would sniff out any gunpowder in the house, thinking it would be mixed with food. Chaney reasoned that this would lead him to any guns that Anne might have.

Chaney had held back Fred's evening feeding to make him more hungry.

Fred sniffed but hardly proved himself a feline blood-hound. He seemed indifferent to his work. Mark wondered whether the "training" he'd given him—all in one day—was enough to produce a result. Still, he kept trying. He and Emil were always daring, he thought, always willing to try the extraordinary.

When Fred meandered into Anne's bedroom, he sat down. Did it mean anything? Or did he *always* sit down in that bedroom? He made some sounds, but Chaney couldn't interpret them.

The cat walked slowly around the room, then suddenly jumped up on the bed. And then he jumped onto a night table. He sniffed around the rear of the table, as if wanting something in the drawer.

But Mark had checked that drawer.

To be absolutely sure, he checked it again. It held nothing important.

But Fred wouldn't budge. He kept sniffing.

Could there be something there? Maybe he'd missed something, Mark thought.

He checked the back of the table. It was an ordinary back of an ordinary table.

The underside was conventional.

Then Mark pulled the drawer out again.

Finally, he did what he *hadn't* done before. He checked the space where the drawer fit.

Of course. Obviously. There was extra space at the rear. And in that space. . . .

Mark rushed back to the phone. "She's got a gun," he reported.

"That comes close to a clincher," Emil said. "Is it police issue?"

"How do I know? They all carry what they want to carry."

"Yeah, you're right." Emil breathed deeply. "I wish this wasn't happening," he said. "Why can't the world just let us do our work?"

"At least we found out," Mark retorted. "I'm finished here. I'm coming right over. We'll develop that film."

He hung up, then crawled to the kitchen to hang up the main phone. He felt the break-in had been wildly successful, a windfall by any standards. It confirmed his suspicion— Anne Seibert had some connection to the authorities.

Chaney now crawled to recapture Fred and return him to his travel box. After that he stretched out on Anne's living-room rug, spent by the tension of the break-in, trying to get a few minutes' rest before sneaking back across the street.

He only rested a minute. Then, Anne's phone rang. He waited for the caller to leave a message on her machine, which amplified the voice through a speaker.

"Calling in." It was Anne's voice, calling in for messages. By pressing a code on her touch-tone phone she could direct the machine to play back all the messages since her last call. There were none, and Mark heard Anne hang up.

Chaney even found *that* suspicious. Here was an active, vibrant young woman, yet there were no messages on her machine. Didn't she have friends? She was free-lance. Didn't she get business calls?

Maybe she wasn't free-lance.

Maybe everything was a hoax.

No, she couldn't put anything over on Mark Chaney. Mark Chaney noticed everything.

He closed his eyes, trying to get that few minutes' rest.

But again, he was interrupted by a ring. This time it was his own cordless phone.

He extended the phone's antenna. Still sprawled out on the rug, Fred beside him in his box, he snapped on the power switch. "Hello."

"Just thought I'd call." It was Anne.

"Annie! How are you? How's Detroit?"

"So-so on both counts. I was worried about you. I called earlier."

"Yeah, I was later than I expected. You know, the usual. But am I glad you called. What a great way to end the evening."

"For me, too," Anne said. "Oh, by the way, how's my little friend?"

"He's right here. I think he's adjusted all right. Climbs on the couch. Watches the cars go by. I don't know how he feels about TV, but we'll try it out."

"I hope he's no bother to you."

"No bother at all."

"Mark, you sound a little odd. There's a hollow sound . . ."

"I'm talking on my cordless phone. It's the reception. Hey, tell me about tonight."

"I said every word I ever hope to say about FSR automobiles," Anne replied, lying on her hotel bed. "All the local bigwigs came to assess our cars, take their notes, and make their comments."

"What's the verdict out there on the FSR?"

Anne laughed. "I'll give you one clue. The standard line going around is that FSR means . . . for the stupid rich."

Chaney forced a laugh. "You could say that about a lot of stuff. But I—"

He stopped. He heard something.

A sudden whirring sound.

Then . . . a bell.

He turned around. He saw it, by a faint beam of light.

Then . . . "cuckoo, cuckooo." Anne's cuckoo clock went off as it struck midnight.

It was a first-magnitude disaster.

"What's that?" Anne asked. "It sounds like my cuckoo clock."

Silence. Chaney's mind raced.

"Mark?"

"Got to get that thing oiled," Chaney said, as the cuckooing continued.

"What? Mark? I said it sounds like my cuckoo clock."

"*Your* cuckoo clock? How could yours be in my house? You saw the one in my den."

"No, I . . . guess I didn't," Anne replied. "Gee, it sounds exactly like mine."

"Well, I think a lot of them use the same mechanism," Chaney answered matter-of-factly, deeply impressed with how he'd finessed the crisis. But it was close. Too close.

They talked for a few minutes more, but Chaney was barely listening. The clock episode had shaken him. Finally, he got Anne off the phone with a promise that they would go out as soon as she returned home.

He threw her a good-night kiss, long distance.

And he started out of her house.

12

Anne lay back, enraptured by the conversation with Mark. She had the room to herself, Carol having been acquired for the evening by at least one man, possibly a squad. She was due back in New Rochelle in two days and started counting the hours. Maybe, if things went right, she and Mark could go on a trip together. Maybe they could even go to Europe. It really didn't matter. As long as she was with him.

It had been such a long, frustrating evening. She still couldn't figure out what had gone wrong with her phone line. There hadn't been any messages on her machine, yet she'd gotten that busy signal. It wasn't important, she told herself, probably a temporary glitch in service.

It was funny, though. She'd always prided herself on remembering details, and yet she really couldn't recall hearing a cuckoo clock when she was at Mark's. She certainly would have noticed, especially since it sounded so much like hers. Maybe the clock's battery had been dead. Or maybe Mark's was the kind where you could turn off the cuckoo. Sure, that had to be it. He'd turned off the cuckoo when she was over so it wouldn't distract them.

Another sign of his interest.

Chaney made it back across the street easily. He deposited Fred in his house, shutting him in the bedroom so he couldn't go scratching at the basement door. Then he prepared to leave for Emil Welder's, carrying the film from Anne's camera.

In his mind, he ran through the list of things he had to do. First, he had to buy a replacement roll of film to put in Anne's camera when he broke in again the next night. Second, he had to buy and install a duplicate chain. And he had to get a cuckoo clock like hers to put in his den. He wanted to be sure she saw it the next time she visited.

If she ever mentioned that she hadn't heard a cuckoo when she'd dropped by before, he'd simply say that the battery had run down.

Mark had no hesitation about leaving his house at close to 1:00 A.M. His neighbors knew that he came and went at strange hours. He walked out to the Jaguar, started it, then slid slowly through New Rochelle, heading for the parkways, which would take him to Emil Welder's apartment in Manhattan.

Along the way he passed several policemen, some cruising, one obviously resting in his car at the side of a road.

His thoughts drifted back to the break-in at Anne's. He had supreme confidence in his criminal professionalism, yet there were always lingering worries about possible mistakes. He worried whether his crawling had left any marks on the carpets. A button might have popped off his clothes. Maybe he'd moved something that he hadn't moved back. He worried whether someone in a nearby house had in fact seen him, although that was the least of his worries. If they had, they probably would have called the police, and he already would have been caught.

He flipped on the radio, tuning in to an all-news station, but there was nothing further about the Riley investigation. These disappearances usually faded into the background, replaced by the latest murder, municipal scandal, or presidential popularity poll.

Finally, Chaney reached Manhattan and crossed to East Ninety-first Street, where Emil Welder had wangled a six-room rent-stabilized apartment for $900 a month, about a fourth its market value. The building was warm, brownish, and prewar, with a relatively attentive doorman. Chaney didn't fear coming in at this hour. The building staff knew him, knew that he and Welder had a business relationship and that they worked at odd hours.

After parking, Chaney walked briskly to the building and took the elevator up to the fifth floor. He had his own key and let himself in.

As usual, the apartment smelled of tobacco smoke. It also glowed with the lights from six tropical fish tanks that lined the living room. Even in high school, Welder had been fascinated by tropical fish, and three of the tanks dated back to those days. The air cleaners in the tanks gave off a constant, gurgling sound that Chaney found impossible, but that Welder found musical.

"Emil," Chaney called out, in a voice not much louder than a strong whisper. But he already knew exactly where he could find his partner. He walked into a small study and found him asleep in a large, leather recliner. Emil, however, had already prepared for Mark's visit. On a desk were bottles of developer, fixer, and Kodak Photo-Flo, as well as a film-developing tank and a chemical thermometer.

Chaney placed his hand on Welder's thick shoulder and shook him gently. "Emil," he said, "wake up."

Welder breathed heavily and mumbled. Finally, stirred by Mark's mild shoving, he opened an eye.

"Glad you're here," he said, embarrassed that once again his run-down physical condition had led him to sleep while Mark took all the chances. He tried to sit up as sharply as he could, the strain of every muscle showing in the redness that flooded his face. "I put all the stuff together here," he said, gesturing toward the chemicals. "Let's see the film."

Mark knew not to engage in small talk. Emil wanted to feel useful, to do something physical as well as cerebral. So Mark handed over the 35-mm cassette he'd stolen from Anne's camera.

"Tri-X 36-exposure," Welder said. "D-76 developer full strength at six minutes, at 68 degrees." He gathered up his materials and took them into a small bathroom, its windows sealed with black coverings so it could be used as a darkroom.

"You need any help?" Mark asked.

Welder laughed. "I can't think of anything you can do in there." He closed the door. "We'll know the whole story in about twenty minutes."

Welder poured the developer into a graduate, measuring out eight ounces. In turn, he poured that into his aluminum developing tank and checked the temperature. It had to be a bit warmer, so he ran the bottom of the tank under hot water. In less than fifteen seconds the temperature was sixty-eight. Then he snapped off the light and checked for light leaks under the door. He found one, sealing it with a piece of paper towel.

In total darkness, using an ordinary bottle opener, Welder popped the cap off the Kodak cassette. He slipped the film out, still on its spool, and started winding it onto a metal reel, slotted in such a way that no part of the film touched any other part. When all the film had been wound, Welder took a pair of scissors and cut it from the tape that bound it to the cassette spool. He was now ready to develop the film.

Still doing everything by touch, Welder placed the loaded reel into the developing tank and screwed back the cover. Then he flipped on the lights and tapped the tank repeatedly to destroy any air bubbles.

He opened the door. "All right," he said, "now you can help. Just tell me whenever each thirty-second period elapses."

Chaney checked his watch and announced each thirty-second mark. Whenever he did, Welder agitated the developing tank to ensure that the chemical was working evenly.

It was strange, Mark Chaney thought, but despite all that he had done—the break-ins, the lying, the wanton taking of human life—he felt a little guilty about developing someone else's film. It was like stealing Anne's family secrets. Maybe these pictures would be intimate. Maybe they'd be deeply personal. Maybe they weren't intended to be seen by anyone else but Anne.

Or maybe they'd reveal what Chaney feared they'd reveal— something that would show who Anne Seibert really was.

The six minutes seemed like an hour. But when they were up, Welder quickly poured out the developer and poured in a chemical to neutralize the developer's action. He then replaced that with a fixer to seal the image permanently on the film.

"This'll take two minutes," Welder said. "Normally I'd wash the film for half an hour, but I'll do it later. We'll look at it wet first, right out of the fixer."

"Good," Chaney replied. He could feel the tension well up inside him as he prepared to gaze on the greatest prize won from his night's work.

A minute passed.

Chaney kept watching the second hand on his Rolex. Two minutes.

"That's it," Chaney said.

Welder poured the fixer into a sink and briefly washed the film, still in the developing tank, under some running water to remove the surface chemical. "All right, here we go," he said, walking over to a lamp. Chaney sprang from his chair to join him. They were like two boys sneaking a look at pictures their parents had forbidden them to see.

Meticulously, Welder removed the reel from the tank. He began to unwind the film.

The first part to come off was blank—the frames following number 14, that Anne hadn't exposed.

But then came the pictures.

Welder held them up to the light.

Chaney studied them. "My house," he said quietly.

"You sure? Sometimes on negatives things look—"

"My house," Chaney repeated. "*My* house."

He walked back to his chair and slumped down. "That tells the story," he said. "It's an ongoing surveillance of me. The only questions are why, and who is Anne Seibert?"

"There's one more question," Welder insisted.

"What's that?"

"How soon does Anne Seibert visit your freezer?"

13

——

Detective Captain Angelo Garibaldi, New Rochelle Police Department, carefully studied the latest intelligence report that his men had prepared on Mark Chaney. He'd been reading these reports for weeks, relating Chaney's comings and goings, but now there was a new wrinkle.

"Who is this Anne Seibert?" he asked Lieutenant Christine O'Neill, who was coordinating the surveillance.

"We aren't exactly sure," O'Neill replied, "but we think she must be working with him."

"Why do we think that?" Garibaldi asked, not taking his eyes from the report.

"We know from one sighting that she visited him in the middle of the night. For a woman who works every day from nine A.M. on, that's highly unusual. It couldn't be a social call."

"No, it couldn't."

"Also, she's away, and we're sure he entered her house last night. One of our guys was half a block away, in an empty lot. He saw Chaney cross the street but couldn't see around to the back of the house. We assume he had a key."

"What's her work?"

"That's another thing," O'Neill reported. "She's working free-lance for a big auto importer. We know from the FBI that Chaney is having current dealings in the auto industry."

"You think she's his eyes."

"Maybe. We're keeping up the watch."

Garibaldi leaned back in his chair, an ordinary police-issue rolling model with worn-out plastic cushions, and rubbed his eyes. He was fifty-one, skinny and poker-faced. Behind him, on a table, were pictures of his wife and eight kids, an American flag, and a small Bible. They defined the man perfectly. Traditionalist, family first, and why did they ever give up the Latin Mass? He'd been in the department twenty-nine years, his father had been a cop in New York City, and his brother was a fireman in Newark. Private enterprise never touched the Garibaldi family, and they felt purer for it.

In only one area did he deviate from basic, conservative tradition: he really did believe that women should work, and should even be police officers. His mother had worked as a secretary to a state senator. His wife was a clerk at the Board of Education. So he had no problem with Lieutenant O'Neill, a thirty-year-old go-getter with a college degree. Garibaldi's own daughter had gone to college and become a nurse. How could he object to O'Neill?

"I'm expanding the surveillance," he said, now putting down the report. "I'll go to my brother-in-law, the judge, and get a court order to wiretap this Anne Seibert."

"Can't the federal people get more involved?" O'Neill asked.

"Federal people!" Garibaldi growled playfully at her.

"They're too busy in Manhattan, where the TV is. Federal people. Christine, we're better than them guys. Twenty-nine years I've been doing this. I know ways."

"I'm sure, sir," O'Neill said. She was a vibrant brunette who'd turned down a chance at law school to get right down to basics, as she put it, and become a cop. She lived her work and had a touching reverence for the street cops like Garibaldi who'd worked their way up by pounding beats and passing civil-service exams.

"I know you just come on the case," Garibaldi told her. "I didn't have time to give you a big briefing. You know the whole story here?"

"Probably not," O'Neill answered. Actually, she did. She'd read up on Mark Chaney and Emil Welder and could recite their lives chapter and verse. But she loved to hear the gospel from Angelo Garibaldi. She'd never stop him from talking.

"So let me explain to you the background," he said. "This guy Chaney had some kind of troubled past—the federal people didn't go into that with me—but they asked us to watch him."

"Because of his troubled past?"

"No, not exactly. That was just an appetizer. He's involved with a partner in some financial company. The federal guys think it's shady dealing, you know, the kind of thing they got on Wall Street. That's why the FBI is giving us information. They're handling the technical side of things. They just asked us to watch Chaney here in New Rochelle. Maybe we'd pick up something, long as we don't go over the New Rochelle border."

"Is the FBI bugging his phone?" O'Neill asked.

"No. Once they tried at his office, but he's got all them antibug devices."

"So it's strictly a racketeering thing."

"That's all it is. I know you'd go for somethin' exciting, like a murder, but this ain't it. All paper and ink. I worry about this Anne of his."

"How so?"

"Single woman. They get into trouble. He probably sucked her into this. Report says she's divorced."

"Yes."

"We didn't have much divorce in the old days. She's prob'ly short on cash. That's how they get involved. I married my Mary Lou twenty-three years ago, never thought of this divorce business. Things are different today."

"I guess they are," O'Neill replied.

"I wish we could follow this Chaney outside New Rochelle, but the law says no. The federals should, but they tell me they ain't got the dough right now. It's small potatoes. They'll get to it." He glanced at his battered wind-up watch. "Better call my brother-in-law, the judge. I want that phone tap. I hate to see a young girl like this get in trouble. I just hate to see it."

Chaney skipped going to his office the next day, explaining to his secretary that he was seeing clients on the outside. Actually, he drove his Jaguar into lower Manhattan, where he rarely traveled, and looked for a cuckoo clock that sounded exactly like Anne's. He found one in a run-down antique shop and paid in cash so there was no record. After that he walked to a hardware store to buy a duplicate of Anne's door chain. Then he returned to New Rochelle.

He placed the clock in his den, choosing a spot that was so obscure that Anne would understand why she'd missed it before. Next, he went outside and rolled the door chain in his garden to wear off the shine and give it a used, tarnished look. He already had the roll of film he needed, courtesy of Emil Welder.

That evening, as Anne went to still another party thrown by Stellar Motors, Chaney slipped back into her house and replaced the roll of film, carefully winding Anne's Nikon to number 14. He also replaced the door chain, using his little, battery-powered vacuum to suck up the wood chips that the installation produced. Then he was ready to leave.

He couldn't use the back door because it was now chained, so he eased out through the front, and maneuvered across the street, undetected. There was no police surveillance that night. The surveillance officers were needed elsewhere, on more important New Rochelle business.

Anne awoke early the next morning. Once again she had the hotel room to herself, as Carol had found accommodations with a young engineer from one of the Big Three automakers.

Anne realized how rested she was, how good she felt about herself and the world. Could it be that the insomnia that had racked her life was fading into her tortured past? Dr. Bradshaw had said this might happen, that defeating the depression could cure the insomnia. She knew, if this miracle was occurring, that she had only Mark Chaney to thank for it. Mark meant happiness.

Mark meant life.

They seemed to merge so well. She laughed to herself as she recalled that they even had the same taste in cuckoo clocks.

She'd gotten up early to find a gift for Mark. She didn't know much about him, especially about the kind of presents he liked, but did want to bring him something from Detroit, and she didn't want it to be ordinary, like a shirt or tie. She hadn't bought a present for a man in some time.

There was a gift shop in the lobby, but it sold the usual

hotel items—watches at full list price, clothing with exotic labels sold at three times their probable worth. And the shop was staffed by people who thought they were doing guests a favor just by coming to work. Anne decided to avoid them and take a walk through downtown Detroit.

She passed a number of stores before one caught her eye. It was called the "Spark Plug," a shop that specialized in gadgets for car lovers. Logical for Detroit, Anne thought. Logical for her, considering her current employment. And logical for Mark, who seemed to have a love affair with his Jaguar.

Anne entered the shop, which was an auto boutique. Counters were filled with cashmere seat covers, oak steering wheels, gold-plated shift levers, and other necessities for the man who really didn't have everything. At the main counter was a guy of about forty, with an enormous mustache, wearing a black leather jacket with a Mercedes-Benz emblem. Anne immediately cautioned herself about revealing that she was with Stellar Motors. She had no patience for shoptalk with fanatics.

"Help you?" the jacketed salesman asked.

"Yes. I'm looking for a gift for a man with a Jaguar XJ6."

"OK." Then he giggled.

"What are you laughing at?" Anne asked.

"Oh, nothing. Just my own philosophy about that particular car—design of the engine, transmission. Don't get me wrong. I know some fine people who respect it. But it's not me."

"Oh," Anne replied. "Well, it's *him*."

"That's all that counts. What kind of gift were you looking for?"

"I really don't know. I'm not much on these things."

"We understand that here. I gather you're looking for something unusual. I mean, not a book on Jaguars."

"Well, a book might be nice."

"We don't carry them."

"I see. Well, do you have anything for a Jaguar?"

"We have very fine floor mats, made specially for that car."

"Well, his are in good shape . . ."

"Jaguar cuff links."

"No."

"How does he use his car?" The salesman regarded her intently, as if this were an engineering problem that had to be solved.

"He commutes . . . and takes long trips."

"Long trips." The mustached face smiled broadly. "The Jaguar travel pack," he said.

"That sounds like something."

"It *is* something. Everything here is something." The salesman directed Anne to a display case in the rear. "This is designed precisely for the XJ6," he explained. "First, there's a compass that mounts on the dashboard. Next there's a cup holder. You'll notice the mounting bracket matches precisely the Jaguar's dash."

"If you say so."

"I do say so. And finally—oh, this is beautiful—we have a trunk rug."

"Excuse me."

"For people with fine luggage. It's a fur rug that you lay in the trunk. It absorbs bumps and prevents luggage from picking up grime. People love it, especially if they carry important things in their trunk."

"I'm sure he carries very important things in his trunk," Anne said. She looked at the set, her eye drawn toward the ivory-colored trunk rug. Mark would never expect her to buy him a gift like this. It was ideal. She took it. She had visions of laying that rug out in Mark's trunk and having him think of her every time he put something important in there.

The perfect gift.

Anne flew back to New York that afternoon, unaware that two men had an intense interest in her—one planning to wiretap her, the other planning to kill her.

Mark had offered to pick her up at the airport, but she declined, fearing she'd look too dependent, too willing to accept a favor. She took a cab from LaGuardia back to New Rochelle.

When she arrived at the house she trudged up to the front door and placed her two bags on the landing. Her eyes went to one spot.

Instantly, she knew something was wrong.

She unlocked the door and threw it open.

She rushed inside, going swiftly through the rooms, inspecting, checking drawers, taking inventory.

Her silverware was there. Some cash she'd left in a drawer was there. Her Nikon was there. From what she could see, *everything* was there.

But still, something was wrong.

She picked up the phone, ready to dial 911.

She dialed 9 and the first 1. Then she stopped. What would she tell the police? How would she explain this? Would they laugh?

She needed advice. And there was only one person she trusted, one person she respected.

Anne dialed Mark's business number. She identified herself to the receptionist as his neighbor and was put through immediately. Mark got on.

"Annie? Welcome back."

"Mark, something's wrong."

"What? Where are you?"

"At home."

"What happened?"

"While I was gone . . . someone was in here."

Chaney's jaw dropped. Where had he screwed up? "What?" he asked excitedly. "Were you robbed?"

"No. I can't understand it. There isn't a thing missing."

"Is the place wrecked?"

"No, everything is—"

"Then how . . . ? Annie, what are you talking about?"

Anne sighed, fearing that she was about to sound crazy. But she had to tell Mark the truth. "I've got a little fetish," she explained. "It's something my mother taught me. When I go away I take a piece of thread and glue it to the outside of the door, across the opening. When I come back, I expect to find it still glued. This one was broken, split. The only way that could have happened was if someone opened the door."

Chaney tried to think quickly, but what could he say? He'd missed something. He'd made a mistake. Were there any other mistakes? He knew he had one immediate priority, one thing he had to prevent. "Anne," he said, "don't call the police."

"Why?"

"Because it looks weird. Nothing is missing. Anne, I know the cops. They'll laugh at you. They'll tell you the thread popped off by itself, or the wind did it, or a dog came up and licked it off. And maybe one of those things happened. But don't sound a false alarm. If you ever have something serious, the cops'll remember this. They may not come."

Anne was sure that the little piece of thread told a real tale, but she had to admit to herself that Mark might be right. "Well, you might have a point," she said. "I'll check the house again. If there's absolutely nothing disturbed, maybe I'll forget about it."

"Do that," Chaney told her. "Look, if you're afraid, I'll come and check the house with you. I mean, you might not want to go down to the basement."

"Yeah, basements kind of spook me," Anne laughed. "I don't know how you figured that out. If you're going to be here early..."

"I'll make sure to be."

"I won't do anything until you come," Anne said.

Anne did feel a little foolish and old-fashioned in revealing her fear of basements, but it sure was a lucky comment. She'd get to see Mark sooner than she'd expected, and she could give him his gift.

Mark pulled up in front of Anne's house at about five in the afternoon. He rushed inside, and for the first time in their somewhat odd relationship, threw his arms around her. "Missed you," he said, as she responded in kind. "You look terrific, even if you think you've had visitors." They were still clutched when Mark's eyes wandered to the Nikon, whose revealing pictures were burned into his mind. "She's watching me," he kept telling himself as the embrace continued. "The horrible, sneaky little runt is watching me."

"I want to hear all about Detroit," he said, "but let's check the house first and get you all reassured."

"I didn't go downstairs," Anne told him. "I mean it, I really *am* spooked."

"You come with me." He led her to her basement door and flipped on the light. "Funny about basements," he said. "Maybe people are afraid of them because they're damp, or underground, like a cemetery. Some people expect to see all kinds of strange things down there. The scariest thing I've ever seen in a basement is a noisy oil burner.''

"I once found a squirrel in my parents' basement," Anne said, following Mark downstairs.

Mark looked around and checked behind the dryer, washer, and water heater. "Looks pretty calm to me," he observed, making a cursory check under the stairwell. In fact, the basement was practically empty, except for some old cartons.

"I don't understand," Anne said. "That thread was glued. I mean *glued*. Just as I said, it's a fetish with me."

"We had a little rain while you were gone," Mark recalled, heading back upstairs. "That could have done it."

"I use waterproof glue."

"Maybe the landlord wanted to inspect."

"He's away. I'm positive."

"Well, maybe he left a key with his lawyer, or someone who watches the property. He could've rung your doorbell to inspect something and realized you weren't home. Look, Annie, why worry about it? Nothing's missing. But, just to assure you completely, I'm taking you through the house."

"Why?"

"I want to absolutely satisfy you there's no *person* hanging out here. And I'm going to insist you change your locks tomorrow morning. Pure peace of mind . . . probably unnecessary, but it's worth it."

Everything Mark said made Anne feel more and more that this was the man for her. He had such common sense, such a feeling for people. He was a *loving* man who would think enough to take her through her own house, who understood her need for reassurance.

And he did take her through. Actually, he rather enjoyed touring the house standing up, not having to crawl around to avoid shadows in the windows. But he was careful to let

Anne lead the way. He couldn't let anything reveal that he'd been through these rooms before.

In her bedroom he did stare at the table where he'd found the pistol. But his eyes quickly shot to something else.

Suddenly the clock—the tell-tale cuckoo clock that almost gave him away—signaled that it was six. "Sounds just like mine," he said. "You were right. They must all be made by the same company."

Anne took him back to the living room and volunteered to whip up a quick dinner. Mark agreed. Why not? Get some free eats out of her before she went to the freezer.

But before dinner, while they were discussing the partying in Detroit, Anne sprung her surprise. "I brought you something."

"Me?"

"Sure, I wanted to. I like to bring gifts from exotic places."

"Terrific! I don't get too many gifts. I guess we financial analysts don't arouse much affection."

"Oh, I don't know."

"Or maybe people think we have everything. We don't, believe me."

"Well, I don't think you have this," Anne said. She walked over to a closet, where the gift-wrapped goody was hidden. She pulled it out and handed it to Mark. "Here," she said, "in celebration of a wonderful day on the Jersey Palisades."

Mark almost choked. Well, of course in some ways it had been a wonderful day. He'd found just the right spot and even photographed it. How many killers were so lucky so fast?

"Shall I guess?" he asked, taking the bulky package.

"I'll bet you can't."

"I know I can't. I shouldn't have volunteered. I mean, a

shirt box gives a hint. A tie box is obvious. Want to give me a clue?''

"Well, let's see," Anne answered. "It's a dark and stormy night, OK?"

"Sure."

"You're coming home after one of those strange trips you take. Right?"

"Fine so far," Mark said.

"You pull in. You get out. And you open your trunk."

Mark didn't answer. What the hell was she saying?

"Mark, you *do* open your trunk. I *heard* your trunk the last time. You must've had something in there."

Jesus, he thought, what is she getting at? Does she know? He just sat there, staring at her.

"Mark, wake up! I think you're tired."

"Yeah, I am," Mark said, barely listening. "Yeah. I open my trunk, Anne. What about it?"

"And you've got something very important in there . . . and it's *thoroughly* protected."

"It's what?"

"Thoroughly protected, Mark, because of . . . this." She gestured toward the box. Chaney quickly unwrapped it, the fur immediately flopping into his lap. A quizzical look came to his face.

"It's a trunk rug," Anne announced, "if you want to treat your cargo like your best friend!"

14

Mark installed the trunk rug just in time for his trip to Washington and his encounter with Frances Burnette. The rug was better than all those blankets he'd been using to quiet the thumping of his back-of-the-car guests.

"I've got to see someone at the SEC," he told Anne by phone the morning he left. "I should be back *very* late."

"How late?"

"It may be dawn before I return. You know me."

Anne was in her office at Stellar Motors. At first she was upset that Mark was telling her about this trip just minutes before he left. But he explained that it was an emergency, something that had come up suddenly.

"I wish you'd take the train," Anne said, her voice brimming with the affection she felt. "I go down there all the time. It's so easy."

"I know, I know. But I love my car, and my trunk rug, and I can't do without them."

He'd said the right thing. Mark Chaney always said

the right thing. "Just come home safely," Anne told him.

"I will. I have to. I've got a family reunion in three weeks."

"A family reunion?" Anne loved those things. "Can I . . . ?" She stopped, but it was too late. She was mortified, humiliated.

"Of course you can come," Mark replied warmly. "I was rude for not having asked you."

Class, Anne thought. The guy just oozed it.

Dumb woman, Mark thought. She'd probably be dead by then.

"Drive safely," Anne reminded Mark again.

"I won't go over forty," he replied.

The drive to Washington was almost routine. Mark had made the run twenty or thirty times before on legitimate business trips. On this one, though, he did take some extra steps. He pulled off the New Jersey Turnpike a few times, drove into restaurant parking lots, even into a car wash once. He had to satisfy himself that he wasn't being followed.

Miss Burnette. Her name, her skinny little face, were burned in his memory. He could still remember looking into those jet black eyeglass frames, attached to a little gold chain so the know-it-all psychologist could drop the glasses to her chest. "You need a different environment," she'd told him in that phony way that shrinks like to talk. He'd always known she hadn't meant it. She'd been one of those insincere ones, the kind who smiled before sending Mark and Emil to that home for disturbed teenagers.

Burnette had been the Board of Education psychologist, an ornament for the community. The school authorities, Chaney recalled, had always shown her off as if she were some precious find. They'd been proud to have a permanent shrink on the staff, especially one so well trained at how to smile at children and talk parents out of their guilt.

"You're not being understood here," she'd say to Mark. "You have special . . . talents that require a different atmosphere."

It had been easy to see through her, Mark now remembered, his teeth clenching, his foot gradually easing down on the accelerator. He hardly realized he was going almost seventy. "I know you have a wonderful side just waiting to come out," Burnette had said. "A little time away . . . wonderful for you."

It wasn't a little time. Mark and Emil spent four years together in that "facility" in upper New York, thrown in with kids who'd killed their parents or robbed churches.

"You must write to me, boys," she'd said, signing the papers to rip them from their homes and toss them into one of those psychiatric cellars.

Chaney finally realized that his tension, his repressed anger, was pushing his speed up to eighty. He took his foot off the gas just as he was whizzing past a Mercedes. Don't get in trouble, he pleaded with himself. Just ride with the pack.

He rolled into Washington late in the afternoon, but before the daily traffic jam produced by homeward-bound government workers. He felt a smile come to his face as he drove down New York Avenue toward the center of the city. He wondered if Miss Burnette ever thought of him, whether she'd ever written about him in one of her research papers. He knew she sometimes lectured on American psychiatric history, and had spoken at the Smithsonian. Maybe, Chaney mused, his case was in the National Archives, courtesy of the same Miss Burnette.

He reached the center of town, maneuvered past the Capitol, then over to the National Air and Space Museum.

Actually, Miss Burnette didn't live in Washington proper, but, rather, in northern Virginia, headquarters of the Pentagon and the CIA. Chaney always looked away when he saw the Pentagon. The army had turned him down on psychiatric grounds, depriving him, he'd always felt, of his manhood. If they could see me now, he thought to himself, a killer, a born killer, someone who handled guns better than a professional soldier.

Chaney then headed for Georgetown, passing the corner of Wisconsin Avenue and M Street, which was just beginning to fill with the evening crowds. He parked in a lot and walked to a Chinese restaurant that had been a favorite of his on past visits. It was early. He had plenty of time to kill.

After dinner he lingered in Georgetown, visiting shops and reading a paper inside a mall. Then, just before 10:00 P.M., he returned to his car.

The trip to Langley, Virginia, took less than half an hour.

Chaney's plan was simple. He'd remembered Miss Burnette as generally open and trusting. He'd simply pull into her driveway and ring her bell, claiming he was lost and needed directions. If she opened, fine. If not, he could get in a window easily. He'd cased the place on previous visits.

She lived on a quiet, modest street that was poorly lighted. Her house was a two-story affair, boxy and unimaginative. As Chaney rode by, he could see a light in an upstairs bedroom window and thought he saw the flicker of a television set. The flicker seemed black-and-white to him, but that wasn't a great surprise. Miss Burnette had always been slightly out of date.

Chaney pulled into her driveway, easing the Jaguar slowly up, almost to her detached garage. He got out, carrying a briefcase with everything he needed, leaving his car door slightly ajar so she wouldn't hear him slam it. He walked to her front door and pressed the buzzer.

He listened. It took some time, but he heard movement on the second floor. He expected to hear Burnette walk down the stairs, but he didn't. Where was she? What could she be doing?

Finally, a second-floor window opened. Chaney looked up just as Burnette stuck her head out. Of course. It was the safest thing she could do.

"Yes?" she asked.

"Uh, ma'am," Chaney answered, "I'm completely lost. Could you possibly give me directions? I've got I.D. if you like."

Burnette smiled broadly, which baffled Chaney. What was there to smile about? "I'll be right down," she said.

Now he heard her coming down the stairs, moving slowly, carefully, the way she'd always moved. Without hesitation, she opened the front door.

"Now," she asked, "just where were you going?"

Chaney pulled some papers from his pocket. "Uh, I was going here," he said, pointing to a spot on a handwritten set of directions. "The light is so bad."

"Then please come in." Again, she smiled broadly. It was weird, but perfect. She was doing everything that Chaney wanted her to do. He squeezed in.

"Show me now."

"I was going here," Chaney replied, shoving the door closed with his elbow, so as not to leave fingerprints. As he spoke, he reached into his bag, grasping a piece of piano wire. "And I made a left turn here . . ."

"Hmm, I see." Burnette was wearing a housecoat, but her gray hair was impeccably combed, and she still had on her makeup. "Well, I think you are lost."

"Yes, that's what I said."

And then she laughed. Out loud. Just as Chaney was easing the piano wire upward. "You expect me to believe that?" she asked.

"Excuse me."

"You *don't* expect me to believe that. Why, you of all people know that I can't be fooled . . . Mark Chaney."

For a moment, Chaney stood there in complete shock.

He dropped the piano wire back in his bag. "Well I . . . what makes you think . . . ?" He could barely get the words out. "What name was that, ma'am?"

"Don't start with me, Mark. I knew your practical jokes years ago. I know you're here to visit your old shrink. Just like you to show up late at night, but I *am* flattered. Look me up on a trip to Washington?"

"Uh . . . you've got the wrong person."

"How's Emil, Mark?"

"Really, you . . ."

"I knew you'd come back some day. We had such a *good* relationship. Oh, I knew you boys would be OK. And you look so successful, with your Jaguar outside. A little time in the facility does wonders for adolescents." Then she grabbed his hand. "Come, sit down on the couch and tell me all about yourself. Wife? Kids?"

Chaney remained dumbfounded. In a bizarre way, he almost liked this. She was so nice. She seemed to care. He'd never dreamed she'd recognize him right off. He'd been ready to identify himself, then give her the speech about justice, about why she had to die. Now he found himself being led to her couch to recite his autobiography.

"Don't be shy, Mark. You sit down. I'll make some coffee and we'll talk. What a wonderful surprise. You must come and stay with me sometime. I asked you, how's Emil?"

"Uh . . . he's fine," Mark said. He still hadn't reoriented himself.

"Now I'll be right back. You like decaffeinated? This time of night, I'd recommend it."

"Uh, yes. Sure."

"Always liked you, Mark. I always argued for you against Dr. Riley. He wasn't on your side—I can tell you that now—but *I* was."

"Yeah, well, it's good to know that."

Mark felt himself softening as Miss Burnette walked into her kitchen. Had he been wrong? Had she really been on his side? On Emil's side? Was she really glad to see him?

Or did she sense what was happening? Was she conning him? Why did she really go to the kitchen? To call the police?

He jumped up and rushed after her.

But she *was* making coffee. She turned around as he entered, smiling once more. "Please join me," she said.

And he did, pulling up a kitchen chair, feeling remarkably at home. But wait a second. This was crazy, absolutely nuts. This woman had sent him to that torture chamber. She'd *known* what she was doing. She'd given him the worst years of his life, and now she seemed to think she'd done him a favor.

He'd seen so few smiles directed his way that he had to fight to resist hers. But he didn't dare return to Emil without her. It was all a trick. Even now, she was tricking him. She hadn't changed at all. She'd tricked him in high school, and now she thought she could trick him again with her phony smiles and shrink lingo.

"You must come to the next class reunion, Mark," she said. "I know you've never gone. But I'll give them your address."

"I'd like that."

She kept up that smile. "I guess the practical joke is over, isn't it? You're not denying it. I never was one for practical jokes, Mark." She turned back to her coffee.

"This isn't a joke."

In a flash he had the piano wire around her neck.

She could make no sound.

She could offer only the barest resistance.

She went limp. Her breathing stopped.

Chaney lowered her gently to the floor.

He knelt beside her and loosened the wire. It had cut deeply into her flesh. "I can't be fooled," he whispered. "None of you understood that. You and Dr. Riley, always plotting, always against me and Emil. Now you can't do us any more harm."

Chaney slipped out to the Jaguar to get one of his large plastic bags, bringing it back into the house. He loaded Miss Burnette into it. As he did, he wondered if she would make the papers back in New York, the way Riley had. Would someone link the crimes? Would it be written off as coincidence that two people from the same school system, now living so far apart, had suddenly disappeared? And would the authorities and the press link those disappearances with that of the judge? These were people who'd lived in the New York area decades before. Most people no longer cared, Chaney thought. And even if the link were discovered, the authorities would find it virtually impossible to track down the murderer. Chaney was confident of that. The superior always were ahead.

He peeked out the window to see if anyone on the street could see the trunk of his Jaguar. No one could. There was a house next door, but its lights were already out. Still, Chaney stared at the house for more than five minutes, searching for any shadows, for any evidence that someone was still up.

And even after that, he waited half an hour, just to be sure that the neighborhood was still.

Finally, he took his packaged cargo out to the Jaguar and loaded it into the trunk, setting it on the plush trunk rug that Anne had so conveniently supplied. He smiled. If she only knew how her rug was being used.

He started the engine and backed out of the driveway with his lights off. In the dark it would be impossible for anyone to identify the car, much less read the license number. Not until he was half a block away did he turn on the lights. Then he headed back across the Potomac to Washington, and onto the parkways leading north to New York, and then to New Rochelle.

The ride back to New Rochelle was pure silk. At one point Chaney pulled into an all-night truck stop for a late sandwich and some ice cream, leaving the car and its curious cargo in the parking lot, but never out of his line of sight. He felt a special excitement about this particular evening, so much so that he decided to call Emil from the road, rather than wait for the return to New Rochelle. He used an ordinary pay phone at the truck stop, exposed for all to hear. But it didn't matter. Mark Chaney knew the words to use.

"Emil?"

"Yes. Mark?"

"Yes. I'm in Maryland. And not very private."

"How'd it go?"

"All the conditions of the contract were met. There's complete satisfaction."

Emil whispered into the phone. "I can't wait to see her."

"You won't be disappointed. I'm looking forward to the meeting. I love to bring old friends together."

"They should enjoy each other," Emil said.

"Quietly," Mark replied. "Very quietly."

Their conversation ended. Mark returned to his table and left a particularly generous tip—fifteen percent for him, and fifteen percent for Miss Burnette.

After all, she *was* using the parking lot.

15

Anne was lying on her couch, clutching the phone to her ear. "I was mortified," she said. "It just came out, but I think I'll be going to his family reunion."

"Hey, kid, don't feel bad," Carol replied, lying on her boyfriend's rug. "So you pushed a little. So you weren't all smoothy. You got what you wanted, didn't you?"

"Well, . . . yes."

"And he didn't hang up, did he?"

"No."

"So don't be so mortified. With men, you sometimes gotta ask. They ask us for plenty. Remember that."

Carol and Anne often spoke by phone late at night, often about the next day's assignments at Stellar Motors. Tonight they were talking about everything, Anne burning time until Mark's return.

"He loved my gift," Anne said.

"See? You psyched him out. I could never do that. Gifts I give—they fall flat. It's great to know what they want. You got talent, Annie." Carol stopped only to look at a wall clock. "Hey, it's late. I'm kicking in. You get some winks."

"I'll try."

"How is that little problem?"

"The insomnia? I think I've got it licked. I've been sleeping, getting on schedule. It's Mark."

"Men are miracle workers. Well, you'll see him tomorrow."

"Before that."

"Before? How's that arranged?"

"He's coming back from Washington around dawn. I know it's crazy, but it's the way he travels. I'll be up for him."

"Now Annie," Carol said, a sternness coming into her voice, "*that's* crazy. You get sleep."

"Oh, I will. But I'm setting my alarm for four A.M. I want to be up. He likes it. I'll make him a warm snack and listen to his war stories."

"Boy, you've got the bug. Well, if that's what turns you on, kid, go to it. By the way, I forgot. His name is Mark what?"

"Mark Chaney."

Carol hesitated. "Hmm. Chaney. Chaney. Why is that so familiar?"

"Common name."

"No, that's not it. Maybe I knew someone with a name like that. Well, it isn't important. Nighty night, Annie. Keep your powder dry. Regards to Mr. Perfect."

Anne Seibert, now able to sleep, set her Braun alarm clock for 4:00 A.M. and went to bed. Maybe, she thought, she'd rush right over when Mark pulled in. She could help him get anything he had out of the trunk and see how he was enjoying her little gift.

She fell asleep quickly.

Perfectly content.

* * *

It was 4:48 when Mark Chaney rounded the turn that took him into his block. The sky was still dark, but he expected to see the first sign of dawn at any moment. He drove slowly down the street, instinctively looking toward Anne's living-room window.

She was up.

Sneaking, devious woman. Buying him gifts. Showing him all that attention, all that concern. What she was really doing was watching him, and he had the pictures from her camera to prove it. But what could she possibly know? She hadn't laid eyes on a single resident of his basement, and she never would.

He waved toward her window. Then, he swung into his driveway and around to the back of the house. He cut the engine and prepared to go through his usual ritual.

Chaney got out of the Jaguar, walked up to the rear door of the house and opened it.

But then he recalled that fateful comment of Anne's—that she remembered the sound of his trunk opening and closing when he came in one night.

He changed his plan. Let Miss Burnette rest in the trunk for a time. She'd keep. Take her to the freezer after Anne had left for work.

He entered the house. The phone rang. No doubt who *that* was.

"Hello, Annie," he said, even before the receiver was up to his ear.

Anne made nothing of the fact that he knew who it was instantly. She'd expected it. "Welcome home," she said. "Good trip?"

"Great trip."

"Everything go all right?"

"Everything. I'll tell you all about it." Then he thought

he'd throw her off guard. Make it look as if he *wanted* her to see what he was doing. "How about now?" he asked.

Anne was thrilled. Delighted. This she *hadn't* expected. "Sure," she replied. "Why not? We've got a lot to talk about."

They hung up. Anne had no way of knowing that this was her first phone conversation recorded by the New Rochelle police. Angelo Garibaldi would get the transcript first thing in the morning and would draw his own conclusions.

A few minutes later, Anne ventured across the street with a tray of goodies for Mark and rang his doorbell. He let her in.

"Hey, that's terrific," he said, surveying the tray. "You didn't have to do that."

"I just wanted to," Anne told him.

"It's appreciated. Very *much* appreciated," Mark said, his warmth shooting through her and making her feel utterly secure.

Mark led her into the living room. He already had his jacket off. His top shirt button was unopened, and his tie knot was lowered. He looked tired, worn out. "I sometimes think Washington is rougher than New York," he said, as he collapsed into a large chair.

"How so?" Anne asked, while starting to serve up some crackers and cocoa.

"It's beyond money in Washington. It's power. Some of the people we deal with down there have a lot of influence in government. They feel they can get away with anything. I always have to caution them about breaking the law."

"Do they?"

"Break the law?"

"Yes."

"Not *my* clients. If they do, I drop them. My partner and I have a stainless reputation, and we mean to keep it."

"That's the only way," Anne said, recalling the scandals on Wall Street. "But I'll bet you know where some bodies are buried."

Chaney blanched, then regained his cool. "Excuse me?"

"I mean, you must know about some shady dealings in the financial world."

"Oh, sure. I've seen some things I wouldn't touch. I've known a few people who've wound up in jail too. Dumb. Just dumb."

Anne spotted Mark's car keys on a table. "Use the trunk rug yet?" she asked.

"Absolutely. It's great. Nothing bounces around. And it's soft. I could put china in there and it wouldn't crack."

Anne then simply seized the car keys and started toward the rear door. "Come on," she said. "I'd love to see how it looks."

But Mark reached out and gently grabbed her wrist. "Not tonight. Look, I'm awfully tired. Give me a rain check, would you?"

Anne hesitated. She knew she could help him. He was sure to have some things in the trunk that needed to be unpacked. "I'll go out myself," she said.

"Hey, no!" Mark shouted.

"Come on, Mark. I don't need an escort."

"No!"

"What's wrong?"

"You don't know which key is right. That trunk . . . it's funny. Jiggle the lock the wrong way and it jams. I've got important stuff in there. That's all I need."

Anne hesitated again. "OK," she said, "you've got your rain check." And she put the keys down again.

"Thanks," Mark told her. But as he eyed those keys on the table, he wanted to kill her. To kill her then and there. To dump her in the basement with the other guests. He loathed her for what she was doing to him, for interfering with his project, for making him worry. He even loathed her late-night snacks. He fought the urge to get that pistol again. One shot. So quick. One wrong crack out of her, he thought, and she'd be history. One wrong look. Just let her grab those keys again. Or grab anything that didn't belong to her.

He watched as she poured some more cocoa.

He barely restrained himself.

The next morning, Chaney waited for Anne to go to work before escorting Miss Burnette from the Jaguar. Fortunately, the cool night air had prevented any embarrassing deterioration. He invited Miss Burnette into his freezer and made sure she was comfortable before locking the basement door and preparing to go to another law-abiding day at M.E., Inc.

But it wouldn't be an ordinary day.

Mark Chaney had made a decision—to carry his probe of Anne a step further, to nail down everything possible about her, to make sure that nothing was left undiscovered.

He called Lisa, the private eye who'd already provided surveillance on Anne. It was only ten-thirty in the morning, and Chaney fully expected to find Lisa in bed.

He dialed her number. She picked up, but only after reaching across her bed on the seventh ring.

"Lisa here," came the familiar greeting, in a voice that sounded eighteen.

"Lisa, Mark Chaney."

"Hello, Mark dear. You always wake me up. I'll have to reconsider you as a client."

Mark was used to it. "Look, Lisa," he said, "remember that case I gave you recently... Anne Seibert?"

"Yes. Not very exciting."

"You let me be the judge of excitement. I want more on her, the kind of more that means full-time for you. Can you handle it?"

"I have some other cases," Lisa answered, snuggled under her pink silk sheets, "but if the terms are right, those little matrimonial investigations can be put off."

"The terms'll be right."

"Then you have my undivided attention."

"Beginning early every morning?"

"How early?" Lisa asked.

"Eight-thirty."

"That's the middle of the night, dearest love. I'll have to charge you the special rate."

"I'll pay the premium," Chaney replied, "for premium information."

"I supply only the best, Mr. Mark. Now, what is it about this lady that so fascinates you?"

"Well, uh, from a business standpoint . . ."

"Mark, Mark, Mark," Lisa sighed. "How long have we known each other? How long have we been together? You know you don't have to lie to me. Don't you think I know this is personal?"

Mark gave out a little laugh, trying to sound as relaxed and suave as possible. "All right," he said, "you win, Lisa. Yes, it's personal, although I don't know how you knew."

"When a man hires me to work full-time, love," Lisa replied, "it's always personal . . . unless it's a major corporate crime. And if it were that kind of case, you'd have told me right off."

"Yes, that's right," Mark conceded. "Lisa, you're worth what you charge."

"Oh, I know," Lisa said. "Now, you were about to tell me why this lady is so fascinating."

"Well, uh, I have a normal personal life, Lisa. But I

always worry about women who get . . . close. You know, when you have money—''

"Say no more. You're thinking gold digger."

"That's part of it."

"And you want me to find out everything she does, how she spends her money, . . . and whether she's digging someone else's gold."

"Precisely. But when I'm with her, I want you to lay off. Don't go anywhere near us."

"Mark," Lisa asked, "would I spy on my own client, my own bread and wine?"

"Lisa, I think you'd spy on your mother."

"Oh, I have, Mark. But you're different. I'll be very discreet. But I'll give you a portrait of this girl that'll put 3-D pictures to shame."

As he put back the receiver, Mark knew that Lisa would do exactly as promised. Sometime, somehow, Anne had to slip up, to do something that would reveal who she really was and what she really wanted. Even if he decided that her life had to end, he had to know what she was up to, and who else might be involved.

Anne was exhausted when she arrived at work. Yawning, she rebuked herself for risking her income on this romance. But she knew she'd do it again, for Mark Chaney was the new center of her universe, and he was worth anything.

She and Carol had their usual breakfast and gossip, but Anne sensed that all was not normal. Carol, usually earthy and kidding, was reserved, almost shy. Anne assumed she'd had a bad time with some man, which was the usual reason why Carol sometimes seemed unhappy, but she also knew not to probe. But, after a time, she realized that Carol was asking an inordinate number of questions about Mark, the

kind of questions she'd never asked before. Had she suddenly become jealous? Had she heard great things about Mark
and wondered why she couldn't have him herself?

Was Carol Trager trying to move in?

"Does he ever discuss his work with you?" Carol asked,
buttering a roll, her eyes never quite meeting Anne's.

"Very little," Anne replied. "He complains about some
of his clients. And he jokes about the hours. But he doesn't
like to bring his problems home. I think we have a different
kind of relationship."

"He open with you?"

"How so?"

"Does he discuss problems? Does he say, 'I want you to
know all about me?' "

"Well, he . . . no, he hasn't said that. But look, we
haven't known each other that long."

"Anything unusual about him?" Carol asked. The question made Anne uncomfortable. Where was the playful
Carol, even the Carol of the night before? Where was the
friend who'd been cheering on this relationship with Mark
Chaney?

"What do you mean, unusual?" Anne asked, now putting
down her coffee, her appetite suddenly deserting her.

"I don't know," Carol replied. "Do you think he's a
straight shooter?"

"Carol, why are you asking me these things?"

"Oh, hey, I don't know, kid. Just making conversation.
I'm interested in men. You never know when to trust 'em;
that's what I say."

"You having a problem with one?" Anne asked.

"No. And I hope you're not."

Anne was dumbstruck by that remark. "Why should I?"

"Look, I gotta run," Carol said. "There's stuff on my
desk." She suddenly got up and left Anne's office, rushing

back to her own without the usual line of advice that she always threw out.

Anne just stared at her as she left. Carol didn't look back. And she seemed to walk more slowly than usual, to lack the bounce that could cheer up a losing locker room after the Rose Bowl.

Anne pretended not to be worried, but she was. It wasn't only Carol's words, it was her tone—not hostile, but probing. It was as if she'd learned something that changed her view of Mark Chaney.

Anne was enough of a worrier without this. With this, she found it difficult to get back to work.

She could see Carol in her office, and at one point she saw her frantically dial a number, speak for a few minutes, then dial another. And then she saw Carol look toward her, realize she was being observed, and suddenly shut the door. Something was happening, and it frightened Anne. She spent the next hour debating whether to confront Carol. She'd almost decided to do it, even at the risk of alienating a friend, when her mental debate became superfluous. Carol came out of her office, grim-faced, walking toward her. She clenched a piece of paper, filled with quickly scrawled notes.

She entered Anne's office and closed the door. "Got a minute?" she asked.

"Sure," Anne replied. She watched Carol closely. It was clear that Carol did not want to make eye contact.

"Uh, I wanted to talk to you about something," Carol began, as she sat down. "Look, kid, I don't like to interfere or anything . . ."

"It's OK," Anne said. "I know something's wrong. Just give it to me. I'm used to things going wrong."

"Well, OK," Carol said. "If you hate me, I'll understand, but if I didn't tell you, I'd hate *myself*. Look, uh, this guy you're seeing. Mark Chaney. The name hit me. I mean, I heard it, it clicked, if you know what I mean.''

"As I said, Chaney is a pretty common—''

"I don't mean that kind of heard it, honey. I mean, *heard* it, like when someone tells you something you'd rather not hear about a guy.''

Now Anne felt the tension welling up inside her, the sense that this was even more serious than she'd imagined. "What'd you hear?'' she asked.

"Annie,'' Carol said, "I used to have a job in the courts. You know, I did P.R. for some judge who wanted to be governor. I think I told you.''

"Yeah, you did.''

"Working there, you get to know a lot of cases. I thought maybe I remembered that Chaney name from one of them. So I made a couple of calls. This guy Chaney, he's in M.E., Inc.?''

"That's right.''

"Too bad.''

"Why too bad?''

"Well, if it's the same guy, and it looks like it's the same guy, then three years ago they got him for securities fraud.''

"Oh, no.''

"He spent six months in jail. He's got a partner, Emil Welder. They went on that vacation together. Then your friend Chaney pleaded guilty to income tax evasion. Big fine, four more months in jail. Look, it was in the past, but I couldn't know it and not tell you.''

"Are you *sure*? People make mistakes.''

"Same personal name. Same company name. Wanna take odds?''

Anne sighed deeply. A mixture of hurt and resignation flashed in her face. "I sure do pick 'em,'' she said quietly. "I seem to have the knack, maybe it's even a science. I had no idea. Really, I didn't. But look, I'm glad you told me. I'm not glad *what* you told me, but I'm glad I know.''

"I'm really sorry, Annie. I hate to burst your balloon.''

"Don't be sorry. At least this one isn't violent. I mean, maybe he wants the eight hundred dollars I've got in the bank. But none of your friends said he was the Boston strangler, did they?''

"No, baby. It's just those financial offenses. Absolutely nothing else. You said he wouldn't hurt a fly, and he probably wouldn't. The question is whether he'd hurt a woman . . . inside I mean. Do you still want him, Annie?''

Anne slowly got up and started pacing the tiny confines of her office, aware of the floorful of people at desks outside who could plainly see her. She didn't respond to Carol's question immediately, and Carol didn't push her. But Anne knew her own instincts. "I want him," she finally said. "OK, I could've done without the news bulletins. I'm not proud of what he's gotten involved in . . .''

"Well, I'm not minimizing it," Carol said. "But they *did* let him back in business, and that's unusual. He had lots of character witnesses. That I know. With people being murdered every day, I guess they felt this was small potatoes. He did his time and he learned.''

"I'm sure he learned," Anne replied. "If they let him back in business, it means they trusted him. Sure, he made a mistake. Anyone can do that. Maybe his partner got him into it. Who knows what really happened?''

Anne couldn't hide how upset she was at the news, but she meant it about staying with Mark. People *did* learn. Maybe prison had been a positive experience for him. She'd seen nothing to indicate that he was involved in anything criminal now, so why dwell on his past?

"You've got faith, kid," Carol said.

"In Mark . . . yes," Anne answered.

"You gonna bring it up to him?"

Anne turned firmly to Carol, a look of iron resolve suddenly crossing her face. "No," she said.

But no amount of resolve could hold back the doubts that began creeping into Anne's mind. She could hardly work. She could barely look Carol in the eye. She began to feel that all the the people at Stellar Motors were staring at her. She'd done it again. No doubt about it. Out of all the men in America, she'd picked another one with a résumé that couldn't be read in public. All right, she thought to herself, what would it be like to be Mrs. Mark Chaney? She'd be married to the most wonderful man she'd ever known, but a man with a criminal record, a man who'd always have fingers pointed at him and people whispering about him.

But it wasn't *that* bad, Anne reasoned.

They were white-collar crimes. Probably technical crimes. Maybe he hadn't even known that what he'd done was illegal.

As the time drew near for her to leave for New Rochelle, she eyed the telephone. One call could do it. She'd told Carol she wouldn't confront Mark, but maybe that would be the best way, the only way, of clearing the turmoil in her mind. Simply ask him about it, telling him the complete truth, that a friend had remembered his name.

Now she reached for the phone.

She dialed his number. Mark's secretary announced her and put her through immediately.

"Anne?" came that warm, friendly voice at the other end.

"Yes."

"Just calling to say hello?"

"Uh . . . that's right."

"Great. You made my day, Annie. You always do."

"I hope it hasn't been a rotten day," Anne said, gaining the strength to put it to him.

"Pretty much average," Mark answered. "No better, no worse than the others."

"Mine too. Uh, Mark, I . . ."

"Yes?"

"I'd like to ask you about something."

Mark sensed the nervousness in Anne's voice, and it baffled him. She was watching *him*. What did she have to be nervous about? He suspected some ruse, some plot. "Go ahead," he told her.

"I was talking to a friend today, someone I've known for a zillion years. Mark, she had some information."

"What kind of information?"

"Sensitive information."

"Oh?"

Anne breathed in deeply, dreading what she had to say next. How would he react? How would he defend himself?

"Anne? You there?"

"It was, uh . . ."

"Anne? What was it?"

"It was about a stock. I just wanted your advice."

16

Detective Captain Angelo Garibaldi read the transcripts of the wiretaps on Anne each day. They made no sense to him.

"These are strange people," he explained to Lieutenant Christine O'Neill as he paced back and forth in his spare office. "Or maybe one of them is strange. I don't know, but I've never seen taps like these here. Now, take the one when she calls him and wants to come over, like, at four A.M. Now it tells me they're involved with something. And these little affectionate remarks. Look, maybe they're close. I don't know.

"But then look at these latest taps. She's makin' all kindsa calls to Washington, to the Securities and Exchange Commission. She wants to know about stock frauds and stuff like that. And she calls the courts in New York for stuff on this Chaney. Doesn't she know him? Is she tryin' to frame him?"

"You know what I think?" O'Neill asked.

"No, what?" Garibaldi replied, a bit skeptical about the

opinions of a policewoman more than twenty years his junior.

"I think she's working with him, but suspects him. Maybe she thinks he's cheating her, or something like that. It's common. You know that. These people never trust each other."

"Yeah. Yeah, that's right. I was thinkin' the same thing. No honor among thieves. I used to know honorable thieves. But not these days. Even a crook is a crook."

"Especially in that stock business," O'Neill said.

"But you know, Christy," Garibaldi went on, "there's somethin' else here. Now, take this talk she had with a friend on the phone just today, couple hours ago. She says she's got it bad for this Chaney, but that she's found out things about him that aren't right. And she's askin' for advice. The way I look at it, she must've known all along that this Chaney had somethin' strange in his past, or she wouldn't be workin' with him. So why these phone calls? And why would she be all bothered about his doin' somethin' wrong back when? And why should she say she's got it bad for this guy when she's probably just a business partner?"

"I don't know," O'Neill answered. "It does look like she carries this act a little far."

"An act," Garibaldi echoed. "Maybe that's the whole thing. Maybe she puts on an act for her friends. Maybe this whole act is designed by Chaney himself. She works with him, then pretends to her friends that it's just a little romantic thing, but that she's concerned about the kind of guy he is. It's a good cover. It's slick. I think she's in his business pretty deep, and the federals tell me he's still scammin' people. That's why we're watchin' him. 'Course, this is all hunch."

"Your hunches are good," O'Neill said.

Yet both of them realized that they were still very much in

the dark. The wiretaps were confusing, and possibly deceptive. And they couldn't know what Chaney was doing
beyond the New Rochelle border because that's where their
jurisdiction ended.

"I alerted the federals about these taps," Garibaldi said.
"I told them, if I was them, I'd put some men on this
Chaney to go beyond our town. You know what they said?"

"What did they say?"

"They said this was small time. They had bigger fish on
Wall Street. Y'know, it's the old story. He didn't kill
anyone."

"I can't blame them," O'Neill said.

"I always blame them."

In the days following Carol's disclosure of what she knew
about Mark, Anne's turmoil grew. She continued to check
with courts and government agencies, gathering all the
information she could about Mark's convictions. There was
little of importance beyond what Carol had told her. He'd
gone to jail for white-collar crimes.

She kept seeing Mark, feeling emotionally closer to him
with every moment. And yet, she knew there was a defect
there, a brush with the law that might say something about
his character but might not mean anything at all. She felt
herself slipping back into depression. Dr. Bradshaw couldn't
help her. He could simply define the problem after hearing
Anne relate her devastating conversation with Carol. Of
course the depression returned, Bradshaw had said, in effect
telling Anne, "You had it before, you've got it again."

And Carol couldn't help. She didn't even try. This was
something Anne had to work out for herself.

Neither of them even vaguely suspected what Mark
Chaney and Emil Welder were actually doing. Mark was so
peaceful, so thoroughly gentle.

Three nights after her conversation with Carol, Anne went to bed at eight, knowing that rest would help her. She was up an hour later. The insomnia was back, the very curse that had led Mark Chaney to suspect her in the first place had returned with its silent roar.

And in her agonizing, waking hours she even took out her pistol, toying with it, recalling that she'd gotten it as protection against her former husband. She could end it all so quickly, she knew. End the depression. The insomnia. The doubts.

But she had too much to live for.

And she *did* still want Mark. She knew him. She knew how superb a person he was. The past was the past, that's all.

She tried to convince herself of that, to have the romantic win out over the worrier.

She had only limited success.

Anne's turmoil was personal, though, and never showed up in the surveillance reports that Lisa was supplying to Mark Chaney. Lisa submitted nothing in writing, nor did she condescend to visit Mark in his office. Instead, she called him each day at noon. Mark would sit at his desk, waiting for the call, for the piece of information that would complete the puzzle and reveal precisely what Anne Seibert was all about.

"Lisa here," the private investigator began one day.

"Yes, Lisa. What've you got?"

"Well, I promised you a rose garden," Lisa answered, "but so far it's only thorns. This is a dull lady, Mark. Either dull or mucho loyal to my favorite financier. She goes to work. She comes home from work. There ain't much else. She's not cheating on you, if that's what you're worried about. And I don't think she cares much about your money."

"How do you know that?"

"I haven't spotted her in any jewelry shops or high-tone boutiques. Usually, the gold digger gets in some batting practice before the final dig. This is Simplicity Sam herself. It's a sleepy assignment, Mark, my love."

"She doesn't meet with anyone unusual?" Mark asked.

"She doesn't know from unusual."

"Keep at it," Chaney ordered. "I've just got this gut feeling you'll come up with something big."

"Oh, I hope so," Lisa answered. "I need more for my autobiography."

Their conversation ended, but it tended to confirm Mark's feeling that Anne might be an obsessive snoop. She might well be falling for him, and she might be the kind, he theorized, who had to learn everything about her man, no matter how she learned it. But if this were true, she could be just as dangerous as any policewoman. For the snoop is sometimes more determined, more driven, and far more sneaky.

Anne and Mark went to the Jersey Palisades again on a crisp, overcast Sunday. Anne thought the weather was ironic in that the gray skies seemed to mirror the new cloud that hung over their relationship. She privately cursed herself for keeping Carol's revelations so firmly etched in her mind. A more casual woman might simply have let them pass or rationalized them away. But Anne could never put anything aside.

The Palisades reminded Anne of their first date and suggested the idyllic life she'd always dreamed about.

And coming to this spot gave Mark the chance to examine again the cliffs that would make Anne's demise so easy, so explainable, such a fitting end to a pesty problem.

They walked arm and arm, along the paths, through the

shrubbery. No one watching them could imagine the divergent thoughts that flowed through each of their minds. They looked like a bland, ordinary couple, and Mark Chaney was determined to keep it that way.

They passed near the cliff that Mark had chosen. It was so isolated, so perfect. And yet he'd decided to give Anne a little more time, time enough for Lisa to complete her surveillance and possibly answer the questions that gnawed at Chaney.

Anne could not help contemplating the cliff herself. After all, she'd already fingered her pistol, wondering why she had to remain on this earth. If things got bad, if her relationship with Mark deteriorated, if more revelations about him rocked her, then a simple jump could end her anguish. It was such a foolish thought, she knew, so unlike her and so improbable, for she'd always faced her problems with resolve. But Dr. Bradshaw had told her that such thoughts were perfectly normal, that most people at some time think of ending their agony. As they approached the cliff, Anne kept staring at it, as if it offered some vicarious salvation.

Then, in a flash, she realized she could hold it in no more. Maybe it was the sight of the cliff and the ugly, depressing thoughts that went along with it. Maybe it was the sudden recognition that only by confronting Mark directly could the cloud pass. Maybe it was the return of the insomnia. Or maybe it was just pure emotion that could not be held back. "Mark," she said, suddenly stopping and pushing his hand away, "I want to ask you something."

"Is anything wrong?" Mark asked. "Annie, you suddenly seem upset. Did something happen?"

"No, I just want to ask you something . . . about things you've done."

"Things *I've* done?" Mark glanced quickly over to the cliff. He sensed what was coming. Yes, she was a snoop, and yes, she must know somehow. "Well, go ahead," he told her.

"I . . . want to know about some activities. Some things." It was so hard for Anne to get the words out.

"Come again?" Chaney asked. His eyes surveyed the area. Could he do it now? Would anyone see him?

"Mark, I like you very much. I think you know that. I more than like you."

"And you know I feel that way about you, Annie," Mark said. "You've brought tremendous happiness to me. I think of us as a great team. But what . . . ?"

"I'm getting to that. Look, Mark, I had a talk with a friend of mine at work. She said she knew your name from somewhere, from a job she had with a judge. She remembered, and checked, and then she told me. Mark, . . . did you go to jail?"

Relief danced inside him. Is that all she knew? Something that trivial? Were all his worries based on those childish federal charges?

He looked away from her for a moment, playing the part of the aggrieved, embarrassed party. "Yes," he told her. "I've got to admit it. I spent some time in prison. I was going to tell you about it. In fact, I was going to bring you up to my office and tell it all, with names and dates. OK, I made a mistake. It was financial, involving my business. It wasn't right, I haven't got any excuses, and it won't happen again."

"It's all done with?" Anne asked.

"Yes. And I'm glad you know. I was . . . influenced by my partner. I should be angry with him, but I'm not. We've been friends from high school, and I don't drop old friends. I learned a great deal."

He approached Anne again and held her arms. She did not resist. "I'm relieved," he said. "I should've told you sooner. It's the one black mark on me, and I think about it every day. Annie, if it bothers you, I'd understand. If you don't want to see me . . ."

"No! I want to see you. I want to be with you. Mark, I'm sorry, I'm so sorry. I just had to bring it up. It's been inside me."

Now they were drawing closer than ever, at least that's what Anne thought and what Mark wanted her to think. "I understand," he said. "Look, Annie, it was a paper crime."

"I know, I know," Anne said, now feeling the relief flow all over her. "It wasn't as if you'd killed someone."

"Of course not."

He'd handled it so well, Anne thought. So direct and forthright. No evasion. No hysteria. No anger. This was a man who *had* learned. This was not a man to be feared or even suspected. "Even if you'd killed someone," she suddenly blurted out, burying her head in his chest, "I'd probably forgive you."

He smiled, looking down that cliff once more, measuring the distance in his mind. "I promise you," he said, "you'll never have the chance."

The crisis had passed so quickly, and Anne realized how foolish she'd been for not discussing the facts with Mark earlier. But the rest of the day was spent in laughter, cracking jokes, walking down from the Palisades, going to dinner at an Italian restaurant in Manhattan. Dr. Bradshaw had always advised Anne to talk out fears with those close to her. The advice worked. Her relationship with Mark Chaney, which she always knew she'd continue, would surely grow even stronger.

Anne had an appointment with Bradshaw the next day. She'd

debated breaking it, because she was sure the heart-to-heart with Mark would end her anxiety and insomnia. But she liked Bradshaw, liked to speak with him about her problems, and decided to keep the date. So, once again, Bradshaw's nurse ushered her into the young doctor's cluttered office, lined with charts, his desk piled with data, professional magazines, and a sample bottle of a new sleeping pill.

"Come in, come in," Bradshaw said in his usual whisper, getting up and shaking Anne's hand. He was in his white lab coat, just back from some sleep experiments that he was conducting on children. "Let me finish this, will you?"

"Sure," Anne replied, making herself comfortable in a visitor's chair. She waited while Bradshaw made some quick notes before putting down his pen to give her his full attention.

"Now," he said, "during your last visit you were telling me that this man you'd met had some problems."

"He had some problems in business," Anne said.

"Ah, and you worried, and the insomnia came back."

"Yes."

"Well, it happens."

"But it's OK again," Anne said, breaking into a smile. "We talked it over, he explained what happened, and I had a really good night's sleep."

"Terrific. But I still want you to keep your sleep-wake diary."

"I will. I've got it with me."

"And you feel you're on your way back to a full recovery?"

"Yes. I think so."

"You once mentioned," Bradshaw said, and again his voice was hardly audible, "that you often saw this man late at night, during your insomnia periods."

"Yes, and sometimes I set my alarm to go off when he comes in late—so we can be together."

"You set your alarm?"

"Yes. Anything wrong with that?"

"Well, for a woman who's had trouble sleeping, I don't think it's the healthiest thing."

"But it *is* romantic," Anne said.

"Yes, I guess it is," Bradshaw whispered, breaking into a tiny smile. "By the way, I don't remember, did you tell me he was a night worker?"

"Oh, no. He just goes on business trips and comes in late."

"How late?"

"Four A.M."

"Often?"

"Yes."

Bradshaw shrugged and seemed to shake out his beard, as if something registered in his mind that he hadn't considered before.

"What's wrong?" Anne asked.

"I'm not sure. Maybe nothing." But Bradshaw leaned forward and clasped his hands in front of him on his desk. Anne had never seen him look so deadly serious. "Anne," he asked, "how well do you know this guy?"

"Oh, I know him pretty well. I mean, weeks, not months. But I *feel* I know him."

"I see."

"Why?" Anne was becoming increasingly apprehensive. She knew Bradshaw was holding something back.

"Does he talk about these business trips?" Bradshaw asked.

"Sometimes."

"In detail?"

"No. He just tells me overall things. But we don't talk

business much. Dr. Bradshaw, you've got something on your mind.''

Bradshaw got up and walked around to the front of his desk, sitting down on the edge. ''Anne,'' he said, ''you've wanted a new relationship for some time, haven't you?''

''Yes.''

''And you know—every adult knows—that sometimes, when there's emotion, when there's fatigue from insomnia, things can be overlooked.''

''Oh, sure. The mistake on the rebound. I've seen it a million times. But that won't happen here because—''

''There's a tendency to accept what people say, to ignore bad news.''

''But I'm not that way. I *live* on bad news. You've seen that.''

''These trips the man takes, they don't sound right. One or two, maybe. But not all the time. Anne, people don't just go through the night like that, driving, unless there's some overwhelming motive.''

Now Anne leaned back and looked into Bradshaw's eyes. An expression at once apprehensive and questioning started floating across her face as she realized that this session wasn't going to end on Bradshaw's usual upbeat note. ''What are you telling me?'' she asked.

''You sure he isn't out with other women?''

The question sent a spike through Anne. Sure, someone had mentioned the ''other woman'' question before, but she'd never taken it seriously. ''I can't imagine it,'' she said.

''I'm not talking about imagination, Anne. Look, I'd hate to see you hurt, but my male gut reaction is that something's going on here.''

''You have no way of knowing,'' Anne said, suddenly defensive and angry. ''He told me—he told me specifically—

that he likes to drive himself and likes the control he has when he makes these trips by car. It makes sense to me.''

''Well, it doesn't to me. Does he own his own business?''

''Yes, with a partner.''

''So he can go into the office pretty much when he wants to.''

''Yes, I guess so.''

''All right. Then why doesn't he stay over wherever he is and drive back in the morning? That's logical. That's what normal people do.''

''Oh, what's normal?'' Anne asked. ''Everyone has a fetish. Mine is thread on doors.''

''Excuse me?''

''Forget it.''

''And this thing about his background. He's gone wrong before. You've got to be careful.''

That hit home. Bradshaw had resurrected the suspicions that Anne thought she'd left behind on that Palisades cliff. Yes, of course, Mark did have that little problem in his past. Was there something else going on now? He'd been so forthright about his time in jail. But he could never be forthright if he were seeing someone else, or several someone elses.

''Look, I think I'm pretty careful,'' she said to Bradshaw. ''I mean, I did confront him about the other thing. This isn't something you can ask about.''

''No, it isn't. But you can always ask to go on one of his trips.''

''I'm not so sure we're that close yet.''

''Assume that you are. Try it. But if I were you, I'd settle this once and for all. I just don't think this man is on business trips.''

Anne fell silent. A few minutes later she and Bradshaw

said their good-byes, he urged her to deal with Mark maturely, and she left the office.

Inwardly, Ann raged at Bradshaw for having been so blunt, for having raised the unspoken issue. Yet, in a strange way, she was also grateful to him. There *was* something wrong with Mark's late-night forays. Mark Chaney was, after all, so relaxed and easygoing. He lived well. He drove a luxury car. Why would he violate that lifestyle with an endurance contest on a business trip, driving most of a day?

Anne was on a roller coaster again. She'd thought she was at the top of the hill before entering Bradshaw's office. Now, as she drove back to New Rochelle in an Oldsmobile that stalled on almost every corner, she felt she was descending one more time. She mulled over Bradshaw's comments again and again. And she weighed his suggestion. Could she ask to go with Mark on a trip? Were they close enough?

Why not?

What did she really have to lose?

"So I was wondering whether you've ever had that problem," Anne was saying to Mark later that day by phone. She was in her office, he was in his.

"Let me get it straight," Mark answered, going over a map of Amherst, Massachusetts, as he spoke. "You pull up to a light and take your foot off the gas, and you apply the brake. Then, when you go back to the gas, the car lurches, then lurches again, then goes dead."

"That's right."

"And all the emergency lights come on?"

"Yes."

"I've had that. Not in the Jaguar, but in some other cars. Here's what you do. Go back to your dealer and have him adjust the idle. It's probably idling too slowly. See if that

does it. And have him check the generator. That could be
giving you trouble. It's probably one of those two things.
You just take it back there."

"OK, I'll do that."

"And tell me how it turns out."

"You *know* I'll do that. Oh, by the way, speaking of
driving, you're not going away soon, are you?"

"Yes. Why?"

"Why? Because I want to start missing you, that's why.
When you going?"

"Oh, well, I've got to go up to Amherst, Mass., next
Tuesday. There are some clients up there. We've got a new
offering on a biotech company in Chicago, and they're
interested."

"That's beautiful country, Amherst," Anne said.

"Oh, yeah, I love it, with all those colleges."

"I'm envious."

"Don't be. It's just a business trip. Not much time to see
the scenery."

"Well, it depends on who you're with, I guess," Anne
said, a little tease in her voice.

"Maybe," Mark answered, making lines on his map,
indicating the location of his next target.

"Got a proposition for you," Anne told him. "A pretty
good proposition, I think."

"Let's hear it."

"Take me with you."

There was an awkward silence. Mark snapped his pencil
onto the desk. What was she after now? Was she trying to
snoop into his business affairs? Was she on to his and Emil's
bizarre plot, and was she trying to frustrate the next murder?
"You want to *go* with me?" he asked, buying time with the
question.

"Sure. Why not?"

"Well, for one thing, I'll be very busy."

"I'll find something to do."

"And for another thing, it won't look very professional."

"I'll hide somewhere. Your almighty clients will never know."

"And you'll miss work."

"I have eight vacation days. Got any other excuses?" Anne tried to sound playful, but she was deadly serious, and she *wasn't* getting the answers she wanted.

"Well . . . no," Mark said. "Look, I'd *love* to have you with me. In fact, I really couldn't think of anything more delightful. But, Annie, it's too distracting. It's . . . it's just not the way I do things."

"Do I have to say pretty please?"

"Even if you said pretty please . . ."

"So it's a definite no," Anne said, abruptly, and with a sudden chill that suprised even her.

"Yes. I'm sorry, but . . . I just don't mix business and pleasure."

"Well, you can't stop a girl from trying, can you?"

"We'll go somewhere else," Mark replied, with many layers of artificial warmth. "On a weekend. We'll plan it. Anywhere you want."

"Fine," Anne said. But it wasn't fine. That wasn't the trip she wanted. That wasn't the nighttime ride she'd hoped she'd take. Mark Chaney had bumped her from that. And now, as she put the receiver back on the hook, Anne could only wonder about the real reason Mark had turned her down. If he were really interested in her, wouldn't he want to be with her, to be with her *all* the time?

He would.

Unless someone else was scheduled for that passenger seat on the trip north to Amherst.

* * *

Anne drove home in the rain that night, her frustration coupled with a growing despair. Maybe she'd been had. Maybe this man she wanted so much really *was* seeing other women. Maybe—my God, she realized, she hadn't even thought of this—but maybe he was even married. Her mind went wild with possibilities, most of them ripped from tabloid feature stories.

What did he do on those all-night trips?

She had to know.

She did have the name of that private investigator—the same name that Mark had discovered during his break-in. When she got home she rummaged through her drawer until she found the paper with the man's name scrawled on it. She recalled his work during her ugly divorce case.

But she also recalled the cost. Anne wasn't exactly cash rich, and she knew these cases could run into the thousands. There had to be another way.

But most important, she had to bring these doubts to a head.

By the time Mark Chaney reached Amherst, she had to know the truth.

17

"Driver's license and major credit card, ma'am."

"Uh, right," Anne said, reaching into her brown leather bag, fumbling nervously for her wallet.

"Take your time, ma'am," the desk clerk said.

"I've got it right here."

"What're you so nervous about? You're only renting a car."

Anne forced a laugh, realizing she was surrounded by other customers at Fast Track Car Rental in New Rochelle, and definitely not wanting to be conspicuous. "Paperwork always drives me nuts," she said.

Sure, the clerk thought, the paperwork. It was always something, always some excuse. But he knew the real story: Anne was just another wife, without her wedding ring, renting a car to go cheat on her husband. It was the usual pattern: the dark glasses, the credit card in her name, so the husband would never see the bill. It happened four or five times a day. Suburban women, bored with their lawyers or investment bankers, out for a fling.

182

The paperwork was finished in about five minutes, and Anne slid into the driver's seat of a new Buick Century. She rarely rented a car, but this was a necessity. She needed a car that Mark would never notice.

As she pulled out of the rental agency, the desk clerk motioned to a mechanic, then gestured toward her. They had their little laugh. They both knew what it was all about.

At ten-thirty in the morning, Anne drove into the parking lot near Mark's office and waited. She knew he would be out soon. This was the day he was going to Amherst, or so he claimed. And this was close to the time he'd said he would leave.

Other cars came and went, Anne barely noticing them. Her eyes stayed riveted on the door to Mark's building, about half a block away.

One car that Anne didn't notice was a baby-blue Mercedes 190, with a telephone antenna, parked in a nearby space. At the wheel was a fiftyish woman with a large, floppy hat. She glanced at Anne, then looked away so as not to be spotted, then glanced again, then went for her cellular phone. She dialed the number for Mark Chaney's private line.

"This is Mark," came the voice at the other end, with only a little static to interfere.

"This is Lisa."

"What've you got?"

"A little lady named Anne, in a rented Buick Century, parked right on your doorstep, Mr. Mark."

"Come again."

"You heard it right. She's waiting for you. I'm sure she rented the car so you wouldn't notice her. My, Mark, I didn't know you went for such aggressive females."

"Just a second," Mark said. "What color is that car?"

"A lovely green."

Mark went to the window and gazed out, returning quickly to the phone. "I see it," he said. "All right, now Lisa, here's what I want you to do. Follow her. Keep me informed of everything she does. I've got to know what this is about."

"You joining us soon?" Lisa asked.

"Yes. I'll advance my schedule. I'll leave in about three minutes."

"We'll be waiting."

Chaney hung up and started for Emil Welder's office but then hesitated. Welder's health was precarious enough. Why upset him with this news before all the facts were nailed down? He returned to his own office, grabbed his jacket and a briefcase, told his secretary he was leaving, and zipped out through a private exit.

A minute later he appeared at the lobby's revolving door. He walked through it nonchalantly, assuming that Anne was watching him. There were several possible routes to his car, but he chose the one that would take him farthest from her. Why make her work any easier?

Then, a sudden, horrifying thought struck him. Was she a nut? Had she come to kill him because he wouldn't let her go on his trip? He knew she had a gun in her house. He'd seen it. Did she have it with her?

But as quickly as the thought had come to him, he rejected it. She just didn't *seem* crazy. The nuts always gave themselves away. No, she was as sane, Mark thought, as he or Emil.

He reached his Jaguar and got in. He started the engine and pulled out of the lot, heading for Route 287, which would eventually take him to I-95 and north to New England.

He checked his rearview mirror. There was a clutter of cars behind him, but he couldn't tell who was behind *them*.

Only three minutes out of the lot, his car phone rang.

"She's tailing you," Lisa said.

"Thanks," Mark replied.

That was it.

That was the smoking gun.

Mark Chaney could tolerate it no longer. He now had absolute, incontrovertible proof that Anne was not only watching him, but watching him relentlessly, even at the risk of being spotted. He also now knew, with certainty, that she wasn't working for the police. They would never have surveillance carried out by someone he would easily recognize.

He got back on his car phone. "I'm turning around," he told Lisa. "I don't like being followed."

And then Mark placed another call, this one to Emil Welder's private line.

Out of breath, hacking from smoker's cough, Welder picked up. "Emil here," he said.

"Emil, I'm on 287. I'm coming back."

"Coming back? Why? This is our dream. We've been planning this for weeks, Mark. This is the finale."

"Yeah, but guess who's joining me for the curtain call."

"No."

"In a rented car, with sunglasses. Right out of prime-time TV. I've got to come back. The finale'll just have to wait."

Anne was baffled by Mark's sudden turn off Route 287. Was he diverting? Getting fuel? Was he taking an unfamiliar route? She'd thought it would be an easy ride all the way, but she'd been wrong.

A few minutes later, her questions were all answered. She saw Mark's Jaguar pull back into his office parking lot. He left the car, re-entered his building, and didn't come out.

Why?

Maybe he'd simply decided to cancel the trip. Maybe he got a call on his car phone that his other girlfriend was sick, or had a headache, or couldn't quite make it. Stay calm, she told herself. Don't create fantasies. Don't assume things. Don't make it worse than it is.

But she was disappointed as she waited in vain in the parking lot. Finally, she just went home.

Welder's office was filled with smoke.

As usual, Welder sat at his desk, his bulk oozing out over the sides of his chair. And, as usual, Mark paced, glancing out the window only to watch Anne glide away and Lisa, at a discreet distance, follow in her Mercedes.

"I'm willing to bet everything that she's a lone wolf," Mark said. "It's all logical. She can't be anything else."

"Unless she is, and acts this way to throw you off," Welder countered.

"I doubt it, but I can't rule anything out."

But Emil had little patience for philosophy. "When will you take care of the problem?" he asked bluntly.

"This Sunday, at the Jersey Palisades. We'll stay at the cliff until there's an opportunity."

"And then?"

"She commits suicide, just as we planned."

Emil nodded his approval, but then the nod was abruptly cut short. "Wait a second," he said. "This whole plan is based on the idea that she's been depressed. But her friends might say that she was happy with *you*. Why would she kill herself if she had this new... friend?"

"I could do a *mea culpa*," Mark answered. "I'd say the relationship wasn't all that close, that she *assumed* things, that I had to tell her I wasn't really involved with her. Hey look, everyone knows that some people get pretty emotional when a relationship doesn't work out in five minutes."

"Yeah, that's good," Welder said.

"I'll even go further. I'll buy some books on suicide and

depression, pay by cash, and plant them in her house after I push her off the cliff. The police'll find them. It all fits.''

"You make it sound easy," Emil said, his many chins folding up like a convertible's roof into an obese smile.

"I practice," Mark replied.

18

___

"It was the craziest thing," Mark said, calling Anne from his car as he cruised home that evening. She'd been home some time. "I'd just left for Amherst, then I got a call in the car that my clients had phoned my office. Meeting's canceled. They want to reconsider their entire financial future. I've never been pulled off the road like that."

"Will you lose the clients?" Anne asked.

"Probably not. I think they're the kind who go exploring, then crawl back."

Anne had to admit to herself that Mark's explanation was logical. After all, he *had* left the office and gone to Route 287. And then he'd pulled off and gone back. Maybe he was telling the truth. Maybe there was no other woman. Maybe she was imagining things, and that Bradshaw had become an alarmist. Of course, she had no way of knowing that Mark was spoon-feeding her this story, knowing that it fit in perfectly with what she'd seen.

They agreed to date again on Sunday. Anne was surprised,

though, that Mark wanted to go to the Palisades once more. She was frankly tiring of the place and assumed he would be too. But this just wasn't the moment to ask questions or make waves. It was the moment to keep things on an even keel, to buy time, to find out more about Mark without jumping to ugly conclusions and, perhaps, losing him needlessly.

She agreed to go.

But, inevitably, she started worrying again that night, as soon as she had time to sort things out, to let the dark thoughts creep in. *Was* there someone else in Mark's life? Would there be? And how could she ever find out?

Insomnia returned.

Sunday was warm, sultry and romantic, a perfect day for the outdoors. The foliage on the Palisades was thick, blocking views, allowing for some privacy. It was everything Mark Chaney could have wanted. Again, he had picked just the right setting for instant death.

Mark and Anne usually visited the area in the afternoon, when they could view Manhattan with the sun in the western sky behind them. But Mark suggested something different for this particular Sunday—a trip to the Palisades in the morning. Why? Because, he told Anne, they'd never been there early in the morning and the colors were wonderful. Afterward, they could explore somewhere else, or go into Manhattan for an endless lunch.

And so they went up to the Jersey Palisades at nine. It was tough for Anne, after a night of only intermittent sleep, but she was still determined to give Mark the day he'd wanted, to talk with him, to probe, to find out the truth if she could.

"It's beautiful up here in the morning," she said to him,

looking around at the foliage, which was an orangey green
in the early light.

"My father always told me to take walks in the morning," Mark replied. "We'll do it again, maybe in Connecticut next time."

"Oh, I'd love that," Anne said.

"I'd love anything with you," Mark replied. He smiled
at her. She felt the old warmth returning. This just didn't
sound like a man who was cheating. There didn't seem to be
anything false about him. Maybe, Anne thought, as they
continued walking, all her suspicions had been ridiculous,
caused by fatigue or the scars of her old marriage.

Mark was looking around, calculating, delighted at how
few people were up on the cliffs. Of course, that was the
real reason he'd wanted to come in the morning. The
statistical chances of being observed at this hour were small.
And the bonus, which he'd also calculated, was that the sun
was in the eastern sky, across the Hudson. Anyone trying to
watch Anne and him from atop another cliff would be
frustrated by the glare.

Mark walked with one hand on Anne's waist, and the
other jammed into his pocket, fingering a blackjack. It
would be helpful to knock Anne unconscious before tossing
her off the cliff, preventing her from screaming. A suicide,
after all, doesn't scream. The bump on the head would look
like an injury suffered in the leap.

Two people were walking from the other direction. As
they approached, Mark put another part of his plan into
operation. "How's that car problem working out?" he
asked Anne.

"I called my dealer," she replied, "and they gave me the
usual runaround. I don't know what I'll do."

"It's not the end of the world," Mark said, suddenly
speaking in a voice that struck Anne as unusually loud.

"You really can't despair about these things. You've just got to put it in perspective and not let it bother you."

Anne was a bit taken aback by this instant philosophy about a defect in her Oldsmobile. But Mark knew that the other two walkers had heard him. If they ever showed up as witnesses after Anne's death, they'd say that they'd overheard this man trying to talk this woman out of some depression, or despair, or something like that.

So far, everything was working.

Mark's arm guided Anne along familiar paths, toward the cliff that he'd selected. He was calm, his voice even, yet he felt his heart pound as he contemplated what was about to happen. This woman was not from his past. She really hadn't hurt him the way the others had. She didn't even know Emil Welder, his brother in blood. And yet, she had to die, for she'd become a threat, a pair of eyes that always seemed to be there, always seemed to be lurking.

"You know," he said, "that's my favorite spot." He gestured toward the murder cliff.

"Why?" Anne asked.

"Because I associate it with you."

"That's sweet. Does it remind you of me because we come here?"

"That, and other reasons. Reasons you might never understand."

Anne knew what Mark was hinting at. He just couldn't come out with it. He was attached to her, but like many men, he had trouble putting it in words.

He guided Anne toward the top of the cliff. Walkers were protected from the steep fall only by a wire fence and some warning signs.

"I hope they always leave this just as it is," Anne said. "No buildings. No development."

"Seconded," Mark replied. "Even this capitalist thinks

developers should be kept away from certain places." He looked up to heaven. "Forgive me for that sin."

Anne laughed, gazing around, feeling Mark's arm moving her closer to the fence atop the cliff. "Hey wait," she said, "not so close."

"Annie, I've got you," Mark assured her.

A bit embarrassed by her fleeting display of fear, Anne now moved closer to the fence. As she did, Mark edged slightly behind her. It was only a matter of seconds.

A slight breeze blew, bringing with it the aroma of the foliage. The view of the Hudson, even against the glare of the sun, was mellow and magnificent.

"We'll have to come here with a little tape deck sometime," Anne said. "Just sit and listen to music."

"Wonderful," Mark answered. "What do you like?"

"Oh, soft rock, show music, the Beatles. I love the Beatles. Every time I think of John Lennon, cut off in his prime like that..."

"Well, you'll get to be an old lady." Mark edged farther behind Anne, grasping her waist affectionately. He quickly glanced back. There was no one around. This was the moment.

He grasped her more strongly.

And... he saw a motorboat passing below and to the left. It was far away, but people in motorboats sometimes used binoculars.

He stepped back.

He wanted no one to report seeing a man standing close to a woman atop this cliff.

The boat passed quickly and Mark stepped forward again. Slowly, he started removing the blackjack from his pocket.

"Do you like boating?" Anne asked.

"Sure. I was in the navy."

"My father had a little boat," Anne said. "Just a

rowboat, but sometimes he'd mount it on top of the car, and we'd go to a lake. I enjoyed that.''

''Well, then, we've got a lot of activities to plan. And a whole future ahead of us.''

Mark inched even closer to Anne. Now he held the blackjack in his right hand and placed his left arm around her.

He cupped the blackjack in his palm.

He started raising it.

He gathered his strength, a grimace coming over his determined face.

And then . . .

The bushes near him rustled.

The colors of clothing suddenly flashed from the foliage.

Voices burst out.

''Don't you move!'' a teenager yelled, and there was as much murder in his voice as there was in Mark's mind.

Anne spun around. Mark lurched against her, discreetly tossing his blackjack down the cliff.

It was absurd.

It was humiliating for a killer who'd planned so well.

And yet, it was so logical. This is what happened in desolate places.

Two teenagers walked toward Anne and Mark, wearing ripped jeans and faded shirts, one of them with his hand in his pocket, fingering a weapon.

''You don't say nothin','' the taller one ordered, his blond hair flopping down over his forehead.

''Take anything you want,'' Mark said firmly. ''Just don't hurt this woman.''

Anne clutched him, holding him close, saying nothing. He could feel her trembling. ''Don't worry,'' Mark whispered. ''Just stay calm.''

''Yeah, just stay calm,'' the talking teenager said, his

partner eyeing Anne, looking her up and down. "You just stay calm and nothin' happens to you." He gestured toward his associate, a little, pimply faced kid of about fourteen, obviously learning his trade. The kid approached Mark and Anne.

"Here. Here's my watch," Mark told him, surrendering his Rolex.

"Nice watch," the little kid said. "Gimme your money."

"All of it," the senior partner demanded in a voice that was thoroughly persuasive.

Mark reached into his pocket and pulled out a wad of bills. Instinctively, Anne opened her pocketbook.

The smaller kid grabbed the pocketbook.

He poured its contents on the ground.

"You didn't have to do that!" Mark snapped, momentarily losing his cool.

"I decide what I do," the kid said, then looked back at the boss for a nod of approval. He took Mark's money first, then went for Anne's wallet in the dirt and emptied it. He grabbed a few of her credit cards and some bills.

And then, like the amateurs that they were, the two kids ran off, forgetting Anne's watch, ignoring the pendant around her neck. One of them dropped a ten-dollar bill as he rushed through the bushes.

In that instant, Anne and Mark held each other close. Both were shaken, Mark not realizing until now just how scared *he* was. They could have actually *hurt* him, maybe even killed him.

Of course, they could have killed Anne, and that would have been more ideal than ideal. Killed in a mugging. The perfect alibi for Mark Chaney.

But even in this, the world was against him. Those kids wouldn't give him a break. Of all the muggers to get, he had to draw the nonviolent kind.

"I'm with you," he whispered to Anne, who still grasped him so tightly. "It's over. It's all over."

"I was so scared," she said, her voice shaking. "I couldn't even say anything. That once happened to me in Manhattan. It was the same thing. I never thought it could happen again."

"They're everywhere. These psychopaths, these people who think they can do anything they want. But we're OK. That's all that counts."

"I've got to report my credit cards," Anne said, suddenly giggling, a frightened giggle, the stuff of foxhole humor. "Imagine, I've got to report my cards."

"I'll do it for you."

"Mark, I thought my life was finished. I really thought—"

"Now, now, it could never be finished because we're together." And he began stroking her hair.

This was awful, Chaney thought. They were alone again, conditions were right, there weren't even any boats in the river below, and yet he couldn't kill her. He couldn't because those two muggers had seen them together atop this cliff. What if he threw her off? What if they read about it in the papers, and they needed a favor from the police? Information is always the best currency for favors.

It would have to wait for another time. Petty thieves, Mark raged to himself. Not even big-timers. Not even the kind who stuffed high school psychologists into Jaguars. Petty thieves did him in.

The shame.

"Let's find a cop," Anne murmured.

"Why?"

"Why? Don't you want to file a complaint?"

Mark patted her gently on her back. "No," he said "They never catch these kids. It's just a waste of time."

"I think we should do it."

"Anne, please, let me just take care of you."

"Take care of *me*? I want to take care of *them*! I won't let them get away with this, Mark. I just won't."

Mark could see that the fear of a moment before was turning to fury.

"It's a person's responsibility," Anne went on. "If we don't help catch them, they'll do it again."

Chaney wasn't prepared for this. What could he do? He didn't want to provoke her, yet he certainly didn't want contact with the police. And he most certainly didn't want some desk sergeant in a nearby precinct taking down his and Anne's name and seeing them together. What would that sergeant recall when Anne's body was discovered later?

"OK," he said softly, playing for time, forming his thoughts. "But I don't want you going through the police meat grinder. I'll go myself."

"No."

"Why?"

"Because I was a victim of this crime, and I'm going right to the police. They may need me for identification."

"Haven't I got eyes?" Mark asked.

"Two sets are more convincing."

"Can't I talk you out of this civics lesson?"

"No. I'm livid at those two."

Suddenly, Mark took a step back from her, quickly deciding on a radical new tack. "I'm not going," he said. "And I'm not letting you go. Period. That's it."

"What? Mark, get off it."

"Anne, I won't go to the police. I don't like police stations. I don't like what they do there. I don't even like the color paint they use."

Although he didn't realize it, he had a look of desperation in his eyes. Anne was baffled and angry. What was wrong with this man? What kind of coward was he? Maybe he was *married*. Of course. No man in that position would want to go to the police. Or maybe . . .

And then it all came together in Anne's mind. She should have realized it. She should have been more sensitive, more understanding. Mark didn't want to go near the police because he had a record. True, he'd committed only financial crimes, but a fear of the police for a man like that was natural. So why force the issue? Why make him go through a kind of mental torture? If there was one way to lose him, that would be it.

"OK," Anne said softly. "If you feel that strongly about it, we'll avoid the police. And you're probably right; nothing would come of it anyway. I guess they've got more important things to do."

"They sure have," Mark said. "There are mass killers out there."

Holding each other close, they walked slowly back to Mark's car and drove away. Each glanced back at the Palisades, recalling the brief terror they'd experienced there on a balmy Sunday morning.

They'd be back again, Anne knew. But it would be safe next time.

They'd be back again, Mark knew.

But next time he'd leave alone.

19

Anne was becoming more and more convinced that Mark was genuine, that his feelings for her were real, and that her suspicions about another woman were probably fantasies. But she still needed absolute assurance. It was in her makeup. The worries were always there, the doubts always lingering, especially when she attempted to sleep. She'd tried following Mark once, and it had resulted only in her trailing him a few miles. But she wasn't going to give up that tactic. She could only be sure if she actually caught him in the act. And that meant following him again, maybe every day, maybe even on weekends. It meant following him hundreds of miles out of town, anywhere he went.

It was simply a question of being sure, of putting the doubts to rest.

She rearranged her work schedule, antagonizing her superiors at Stellar Motors, something she'd never have done if there were no Mark. And she opened accounts at a variety of car rental agencies. She was afraid of frequenting the same one all the time. They'd become suspicious, she thought. They'd think she was a wife cheating on her husband.

"She's back," Lisa reported one day, as she spied Anne in the parking lot outside Mark's office.

"What's she got today?" Mark asked.

"Looks like a Ford Taurus, silver, red upholstery. Four-door sedan. Nice job. Want to buy a used car, Mr. Mark?"

"Not from Anne Seibert, or her rental agency. I'd love to know who's paying for those cars."

"My people tell me it's her."

"Maybe," Mark said. "Or maybe she's got someone on the side."

"My, my, how jealous we are."

"Don't bet on it, Lisa. She doing anything unusual?"

"No. Just coming here . . . and waiting."

"No camera?"

"No camera, no car phone. Just her and her eyes."

The ritual of Anne's waiting outside Mark's office went on day after day. Mark would leave the office, avoid looking in Anne's direction, get into his car, and drive home slowly. Anne would always follow three or four car lengths behind, traveling in a different lane so she could observe Mark at an angle. She would break off just as they entered New Rochelle. Then she'd go to a phone booth and call him at home, just to make sure he was there.

One afternoon, though, after Anne called, Mark was relaxing in his living room when a bizarre thought hit him. It was something, incredibly, that he hadn't considered before, and the lapse embarrassed him, angered him, for he was not a man to tolerate his own mistakes.

He thought back to the night he'd broken into her house and found her gun. Why did she have that gun? He'd given it only brief thought at the time, then forgotten it. He'd theorized that it was logical for someone doing official surveillance to be armed, but what if she wasn't doing official surveillance? And why wouldn't she carry it with her?

Other people had guns.

Other kinds of people.

He went for his phone to call Emil Welder, who was still in the office at M.E., Inc. Emil, surrounded as usual by billowing smoke, saw his private line light up and answered immediately.

"This is Emil."

"Emil," Mark said, "I may have something. Are you alone?"

"Yes."

"I just had a terrible thought. I mean, really terrible."

"Let's have it."

"Maybe this Anne Seibert is one of us."

Welder winced, his puffy face folding over into a ripply lump of dried fruit. "What do you mean, one of us? One of whom?"

"Someone who's involved in something. The way we're involved in something."

Emil Welder knew exactly what Mark meant. "Odd," he said, "with our kinds of minds, we should have thought of that sooner."

"Yes. Much, much sooner. But it all fits. Maybe we're being targeted by someone. It might be a competitor, or maybe some ring somewhere. They may want to muscle in on M.E., Inc. Maybe they want to get rid of us entirely. And they'd think we'd never suspect a next-door neighbor."

"How do we find out what's true here?" Welder asked.

"We don't. I've had her followed, and she's clean on the surface. If she's reporting back, she's doing it at work, or by mail. Lisa can't cover her twenty-four hours a day. Look, this could be wrong, but it could be very right. The lady has a gun. I don't know how she plans to use it."

"I'm upset by these thoughts," Emil said.

"I'll just be careful," Mark assured him. "I tried to remove her once. It didn't work. I'll try again in a few days."

"Same spot?"

"Yes. I asked her when she called before. She had some little complaint about going back there—you know, to where we got mugged. But I told her that's exactly why we should go."

"Like getting right back on a horse after you've been thrown," Welder said.

"Yes, that's it."

"I know it'll work this time," Emil replied. "And Mark, are you ready for tomorrow night?"

"I'm almost ready," he said. "I'll leave my office at three P.M. for Amherst."

"But she'll follow you."

"I'm working that out. If she succeeds again, it's another washout. But she won't succeed."

"Have you told her you're taking the trip?"

"No. I'll tell her later. I don't want to give her too much time to think about it."

At that moment, someone opened the door to Emil's office and rushed in, holding a stock bulletin. "I'll talk to you later," Emil said to Mark. Their privacy destroyed, they both abruptly hung up.

Mark lay back on his couch and thought about his latest theory. As he did, he became haunted over the possibility that it was actually right. It was bad enough, he mused, to be watched, studied, to have those searching eyes on him, sometimes in the middle of the night. But to be watched by someone who might be part of some criminal group was the lowest of low blows to someone who killed regularly, and superbly.

The nerve.

The arrogance.

The phoniness of the woman.

There was something sleazy about this kind of deception that revolted Mark. *He* killed those who had hurt him—people who deserved to die, who'd deserved to die years ago. What was Anne's motive? Money for some group? Power?

He stopped himself. He knew how his imagination could run free, and now it was running out of control. After all, this was only a theory.

He had to tell Anne about his new trip to Amherst. He reached for the phone.

Anne was in a bright red housecoat, having just stepped out of the shower. She let the phone ring twice, as was her habit, then picked up.

"Hello?"

"Hi."

"Mark. I didn't expect you. I spoke to you only an hour ago."

"I forgot to tell you something," Mark replied. "Actually, I was trying to put it out of my mind."

"What happened?"

"Well, it's good news and bad news. The good news is, we've patched things up with my clients in Amherst. The bad news is, I've got to go up there tomorrow."

"We'd planned to be together tomorrow night," Anne replied, her voice dropping.

"Yeah, I know. I tried to get out of it, or put it off a week. But it's a major account. I don't see where I have much choice. I'll miss you, Annie."

"I'll wait up for you."

"No, you won't!"

"I certainly will."

"Oh, come on. Anne, you've got to break that habit. You'll ruin yourself. I'll call you the next morning."

"We'll see," Anne teased. But the teasing in her voice belied the fright she suddenly felt. He was going away again. Where? To that other woman? He'd started out on the Amherst trip the previous week, only to return. But who knew what the truth was, where he'd really been heading? "Are you leaving late?" she asked.

"Well, late afternoon. About three."

"Can I help you with anything?"

"You're sweet to ask," Mark said, "but I think I'm pretty much set. You know, I'm always ready to travel. I've even got suits in the office."

"Remember," Anne said, "you promised that you'd take me on one of these trips."

"The promise will be kept," Mark replied. Sure, it would. Anne would be accompanying him on a trip that very weekend, to the Jersey Palisades.

"Call me from Amherst?" she asked, then realized that wasn't so wise. She wouldn't be home. She'd be following him.

"Sure," Mark replied. "Let's say, sometime around seven?"

"Fine. If I have to work late, leave a message on my machine."

Mark hung up, but Anne simply pressed the button on her telephone and made another call—to a car rental agency in White Plains. She'd need a car for the next day, and one that was fuel-efficient. She didn't want to stop for gas if she was going to trail Mark all the way to Amherst.

Inside, she had a gut feeling that this trip would reveal everything.

It would all come out in Massachusetts.

20

___

The day of the Amherst trip was darkened by thunderstorms, which was exactly the way Mark Chaney liked it. He called Massachusetts weather information from his home in the morning and learned that the storms extended all the way up into Amherst. God was on his and Emil's side, as he had always assumed. Everything would be ideal for the last murder in the project—a doubleheader in Amherst, two people whom he loathed more than any of the others.

He packed a silencer-equipped pistol into the spare-tire well of the Jaguar, and a roll of piano cord into the glove compartment. He carried ammunition in an asbestos-lined box on the front seat. Chaney insisted on a fireproof box out of fear that, in a collision, his car would catch fire and the ammunition would explode. He also brought two "lawn 'n leaf" plastic bags, his standard merchandise container. And he removed a box of tools from the trunk to make room for the two guests he expected to have on the return trip.

He left his house for his office at 1:00 P.M. There was no point in going in earlier, as his mind was most certainly not on M.E., Inc. As he left New Rochelle in a driving rain, he had a sense of exhilaration he hadn't felt since murdering his former music teacher almost a year before.

Tonight was going to be the highlight of his life.

Anne watched from the side of her bedroom window as Chaney left. She'd arranged to have the day off and went immediately to a phone to call the car rental agency.

"This is Anne Seibert," she said. "Is my car ready and fueled?"

"Yes, ma'am."

"And it's the Ford Tempo?"

"Yes, ma'am. Just like you ordered."

"I'll be there in ten minutes."

Good. The Tempo got great mileage.

Anne called a cab to take her to the rental agency. She'd already packed a small bag with all the things she'd need for the trip, including her camera and telephoto lens. She also made sure she had her large sunglasses, which effectively hid her face.

The cab arrived. Anne headed off. Lisa was observing from about a block away and started following the cab. She'd also taken to renting cars, at Mark's expense of course, for fear that Anne would notice that same Mercedes near her day after day. Today Lisa had a BMW, with a bar and car phone. When Lisa rented, Lisa rented in style.

"All right, she's here again," Lisa reported, just after Anne pulled into Mark's parking lot. "A cheap Ford Tempo, sickly brown with yellow upholstery. She's wearing a gray dress and oversized sunglasses. Very CIA.''

"Got you," Mark replied, looking right at Anne's car from his office window. He could barely see it through the rainstorm, and a lightning bolt almost wiped out Lisa's last sentence. But he was well briefed and ready for the chase that would start at three. "You might as well go home," he told Lisa. "I'll take it from here."

He watched the clock and studied a map of White Plains, making sure he had his directions and street names absolutely right. Then, at five minutes of three, he walked slowly into Emil's office, closing the door behind him.

"Just saying good-bye," Mark said.

Emil, hunched over in his desk chair, stared at his partner for a moment, then struggled to rise. He hobbled over to Mark, and without a word, embraced him. He'd never done that before, but Mark understood what his partner was experiencing at that moment. He shared the emotion, the sense of impending victory. "Good luck," Emil said. "I can't wait for your call."

"I'll phone as soon as possible," Mark told him. "Emil, we're almost at the end. All those people who hurt us, who took away our young years, they'll all be . . .''

"And we've done it ourselves," Emil said.

They embraced again. And then Emil reached into his pocket, took something out, and pressed it into Mark's hand. Mark looked down. Crumpled in his palm was a small article from his high-school newspaper. The headline read "TWO STUDENTS CHARGED."

"You've kept it all these years," Mark said.

"Yes. I look at it all the time, just to remember how it felt. It keeps the anger going."

"What shall I do with it?"

"Take it to Amherst. Show it to them. Let it be the last thing they see."

Mark smiled and stuffed the little article into his jacket pocket.

He returned to his office, grabbed a briefcase and a black Knirps umbrella, and left the headquarters of M.E., Inc. He rode down alone in the elevator, emerging from the building a few minutes later. He stepped outside and snapped open the umbrella.

Out of the corner of his eye he could see Anne, squeezed down in her seat, staring at him through those oversized sunglasses. He fought to avoid staring back; instead he walked briskly toward his Jaguar, which was slick and streaked from the drenching rain.

He reached his car, instinctively examining it for any signs that it had been broken into. He got in and started the engine.

Mark heard Anne's Ford start some forty yards away. He moved to adjust his rearview mirror, momentarily tilting it all the way to the left to get a better view of the Ford and its occupant.

Chaney started to pull out, his windshield wipers flapping back and forth, his electric rear defroster quickly clearing the window of fog. He left the parking lot and headed toward White Plains.

Anne followed, immediately baffled by the direction. This wasn't the usual way north to Massachusetts. Was it a new route? Or was Mark planning to pick up something in White Plains before heading for Amherst? Had he detected her? Was he maneuvering to get away?

Mark entered White Plains, cruising down Route 22, past Alexander's department store, past Harvey Sound; then he made a right turn onto Mamaroneck Avenue, one of the town's busiest shopping streets. It was congested, but Mark suddenly lurched ahead, zipping around cars, once crossing the double yellow line and moving down the wrong side of the street.

Anne had trouble keeping up. For a moment, she lost Mark in the rain's reflections. The she saw him again, lost him, then saw him.

She heard angry drivers honking at Mark. She couldn't figure why he was suddenly doing this. She followed him around a corner, then into a side street, then around another corner.

And then Mark pulled into an alley. He seemed familiar with it, but Anne wasn't. She got a glimpse of him zipping out of the alley, then through a parking lot behind some stores. She tried to follow, but a car coming in the other direction, down that narrow alley, stopped her. She had to back out and let the other driver through.

Then she sped down the alley.

She charged into the parking lot, drawing a furious glance from an attendant.

Her eyes swept the area.

No Mark.

No Jaguar.

She looked for the exits. There must have been five of them, pouring onto three separate streets. Anne's insides began to tighten as she contemplated what had happened.

She rolled down her window, waving wildly toward the parking attendant, a red-haired kid of eighteen who still had that angry, I-hate-dumb-drivers look. "Hey," she shouted, "did you see a red Jag go by here?"

"Yeah," he answered, utterly nonchalant.

"Just a minute ago?"

"Yeah."

"Where'd he go?"

"How would I know, lady? He didn't check in with me. Know what I mean?"

Anne fought to keep her cool, to avoid insulting him. "All I'm asking is, what exit did he take? What street did he go out on?"

"Which are you asking?" the kid wanted to know.

"Either question."

"I wasn't looking."

"Thanks," Anne said, rolling her window back up.

"Any time."

Anne paused a few moments, again sweeping the parking lot with her searching eyes. No red Jaguar. Mark had eluded her, whether intentionally or not. She could only guess which road he'd taken.

She headed out of the lot, winding her way onto Main Street. She flipped a coin in her head and chose a northerly course, assuming Mark would have to head north eventually to get on the routes to Amherst.

But she couldn't find him.

After searching for an hour, she simply decided to pull over to a curb and think it through. She could give up, she knew, or she could go to Amherst by herself, hoping to spot Mark up there.

Eventually she simply decided to give up, at least for this trip. Going on a wild-goose chase was simply too demeaning, too foolish. And not finding Mark in Amherst would be too discouraging. There'd have to be other chances to follow him, to learn the truth. Disheartened, drained, she started her rented car again, pulled out into traffic, and drove back to the rental agency.

The sign said "Hartford, 20 miles."

Mark had been driving with his eyes alternating between the road and the rearview mirror. Now, getting deep into Connecticut, he was sure he'd lost Anne. He relaxed a bit, glancing over at the box of ammunition on his front seat. He was pleased with the work he'd done. With Anne off his tail he had the independence to do the rest of the job.

He needed one final piece of assurance, so he reached for his car phone and tapped in Anne's number. The phone in her house rang two times, then he heard the receiver being taken off the hook.

"Hello," Anne said.

He hung up. He felt like a teenager playing telephone games.

Angelo Garibaldi had gone beyond reading the transcripts of Anne's daily calls. Now he listened to them on a speaker hookup in his office. An officer would alert him when Anne picked up the phone, and he would snap on his equipment. Tracing devices told him within seconds where the call was coming from.

"Listen to this," he said to Christine O'Neill, as she walked into his office while one of Anne's calls was in progress. "She's talkin' to a friend."

Anne was speaking with Carol Trager, and she sounded near tears.

"I don't know if it was intentional," she was telling Carol, as Garibaldi and O'Neill listened intently. "But he whizzed up this alley and then out the other side of a parking lot. Maybe he saw me. I don't know. But he never went that way before in all the times I've been watching him."

"Kid, maybe you better stop watching," Carol said. "Give him up. He's makin' you nuts."

"Carol, you play both sides of the street."

"I sure do, baby. That way you've always got a sidewalk

to walk on. Sounds to me like he spotted you and then tried to shake you.''

''Why?''

''Why? You guess why. I think he's got a whole corporation full of women, and I'm not sure they're in Massachusetts.''

''I don't think I could stop seeing him without finding out for sure,'' Anne said. ''I'd hate myself. I don't get these chances too often, and—''

''So keep seeing him. But you'll have to get closer. *Demand* to go on his next trip. Don't just request.''

''I had one idea,'' Anne said, sitting hunched over on a kitchen chair, still deflated by the afternoon's experience. ''I could call his office and say I had to talk to him. I could ask for his number in Amherst. At least I'd know whether he's actually there.''

''Annie, this is what I mean. You're beginning to get crazy. That's what kooks do. Even this following him. It isn't worth it. No man is worth it.''

''Maybe I'll call my doctor,'' Anne said.

''What'll he tell you? Take two sleeping pills and call him in the morning? Look, this isn't you. You went through this miserable divorce. You were like iron. Independent. Gutsy. I don't like what's happening now.''

''Neither do I.''

''Give yourself a deadline. Get him in a room, and tell him you've never known a man to take these long trips and come back the same night. And tell him you're a little bit worried. And tell him you'll be in his passenger seat next time. If he balks, you walk.''

''Maybe you're right.''

Garibaldi and O'Neill listened, each thoroughly baffled. ''It could still be some kind of cover,'' Garibaldi said. ''I mean, she could be makin' this all up. We still haven't got a fix on exactly what these two do together.''

"And maybe it's real," O'Neill said.

"You know, Chrissie, I'm beginnin' to think that might just be the case. Just a hunch, that's all. They could work together, but maybe they've got this thing goin' on the side. I wish the federals would take this over. Oh, by the way, they told me the U.S. attorney has this Chaney hooked to mail fraud."

"Is she involved?"

"They don't know. But if he gets pulled in, she'll have her name all over page one. If she's involved or not, she'll have problems. It's who you hang out with."

"When is the U.S. attorney moving in?" O'Neill asked.

"Tomorrow. He brings Chaney in for questioning."

As she lay on her couch contemplating Carol's advice, Anne felt the knot in her stomach that often accompanied the onset of depression . . . and insomnia. She knew she wouldn't be able to sleep. She knew she wouldn't be able to concentrate on any of the work she had brought home from Stellar Motors. She could only stare at the ceiling and think about Mark. Everything was Mark. Nothing else in life seemed to matter.

Very easy for Carol to give advice, she mused. Carol wasn't her, and Carol didn't understand how terrific it felt just to be with Mark Chaney. Carol seemed to attract men like flies, some with an intelligence to match.

But maybe Carol was right about just one thing. Maybe it was time simply to confront Mark, to demand to go with him on his next trip. He would be coming back early in the morning, and maybe that would be just the time to broach the subject. She'd be up, he'd understand her anxiety, maybe he'd finally come clean and reveal what these trips were about.

Anne felt she couldn't go on like this, feeding her tendency toward obsessive worry.

But would she have the guts to confront Mark tonight, when he came home?

She really didn't want to.

She knew it could end in an explosion, and a collapse of their relationship.

But she had to act. This was destroying her.

She lay there and made up her mind.

21
___

Chaney set the Jag on cruise control, and the car automatically maintained a sixty-mile-per-hour speed with his foot off the accelerator. He knew that, if he could avoid traffic jams, the trip to Amherst would take less than three hours.

He wondered what those two were thinking. Did they have any idea that this was their last day on earth? Had they prepared? Did they have a will? Life insurance for their children? Did they ever discuss death with each other, or were they these giddy types who never thought about anything unpleasant? Chaney vaguely recalled them as being the ultraresponsible type who would have their papers in order and their beneficiaries listed down to the last nephew. Solid citizens.

The sun broke through the storm clouds in the western sky, creating some glare whenever the road twisted left. Chaney occasionally flipped down the visor but saw some drivers start to weave, unable to get their bearings in the face of the bright light.

Suddenly, he saw a silver 1985 Buick lurch out of its lane. It came so close to a Nissan that the Nissan's driver swerved to avoid an accident, running off the road, rumbling along the shoulder.

Desperate to get back on the pavement, the Nissan swerved left, but as its wheels hit the road the car careened out of control.

It piled into a station wagon.

The two cars locked. At sixty miles an hour.

The wagon turned over, bursting into flame.

Chaney swerved to avoid the wreck, but the Nissan caught his side, and the Jaguar shook with the impact.

He momentarily lost control but quickly regained it. He immediately pulled over to the side and screeched to a halt.

He looked back.

The wagon was on fire, but its driver had escaped.

The Nissan was totaled, its driver and a passenger trapped inside.

Already, Chaney could see a Connecticut state patrol car, its red lights flashing, speeding to the accident.

Cars were careening around the wreck, and now some were stopping, their drivers rushing to give aid. Traffic began to pile up. The inevitable horns started to honk, drivers far back not realizing what had happened.

Chaney thought of leaving. He had important work to do, more important than hanging around this mess. But he knew someone might have seen him, might have caught his license number. He could be reported for leaving the scene of the accident, and that would bring the police to his home with a summons, or maybe even a warrant. They'd run him through the computer and realize he had a record.

No, he had to stay. He had to play the game. He even had to fill out forms. He had to do anything to avoid an unfriendly attitude on the part of the police.

The damage to the Jaguar was minor—an unsightly scrape along the left side extending from the front fender to the rear door. Nothing that would interfere with the trip to Amherst.

He rushed back to the accident. No one could get close to the burning wagon, but no one remained inside. The Nissan's passengers, a young man and young woman, were struggling unsuccessfully to get out. They were cut and bruised, but didn't seem that badly hurt, despite the condition of their car. Chaney gestured for the approaching Connecticut patrolmen to concentrate on getting them out.

An ambulance and tow truck came quickly. It took about ten minutes for the tow-truck operator, using a crowbar, to free the Nissan's passengers. Both were placed on stretchers and whisked to a hospital, in pain but fully conscious.

It was a miracle, people were saying, that no one had been killed.

Seat belts, a few murmured. The people in the Nissan had been wearing their seat belts.

A few people commiserated with Chaney and inquired as to whether he was injured. He wasn't. One of the Connecticut troopers, a powerfully built, ruddy-faced officer with reflecting sunglasses, approached him, carrying a clipboard. "Uh, I hear you witnessed the whole thing," he said, in a tight voice that was too high for the man's size.

"I did, Officer," Chaney replied, on his best Boy Scout behavior. "My car got scraped."

"You want medical aid?"

"No, I'm all right."

"Sure? Didn't get hit in the head, did you?"

"No, Officer. I got scraped on the side."

"Head injuries show up later," the trooper said. "If you banged your head, you gotta tell me. I don't want my boss askin' questions if you die later."

That was certainly warm and kind, Chaney thought. "I didn't hit my head, Officer," Chaney said. "I just got jostled."

"Maybe I should take you to the hospital," the cop said. "You lie down."

"No, now wait, I'm OK. I'll sign a release. I'll say I'm all right."

The officer looked Chaney up and down, assessing him, looking for any blood or sign of bodily damage. "All right, I want that release, in triplicate. Now, I hear there was another car involved."

"That's right A silver Buick. Late model."

"Get its license?"

"No, I'm afraid not. But he caused it, then ran off."

"I'll radio ahead. They'll stop him somewhere. That car have any distinguishing marks that you saw? College stickers? Bumper stickers? Dents?"

"Not that I recall."

"Catch a look at the occupants?"

"I just saw the driver. Male. Maybe forty years old."

"Would you recognize him if you saw him again?"

Chaney hesitated, pretending to think about the question. Actually, he was trying to figure out how he could get away. "No, it happened too fast," he said.

"That your car?" the officer asked, pointing to the Jaguar.

"Right."

"Jag. You get it new?"

"Uh, yes I did."

"My brother's got a Jag," the officer said. "Cost him forty grand."

"Yes," Chaney said. "They are expensive."

"Not worth it, as far as I'm concerned. I mean, four wheels is four wheels. A Chevy gets you there just as fast."

"Certainly does, Officer."

"That damage'll cost you big bucks. You or your insurance company. Jaguar. They know how to charge."

"I've noticed that," Chaney replied. He just wanted to get out of there. He'd sign anything, but he wanted to go. But, without another word, the trooper started walking toward the Jag, his brown uniform flapping in the breeze. "I gotta write this here damage up," he said.

Chaney followed, always apprehensive about any policeman coming near his car. After all, it was a rolling arsenal, and the ammunition box was fully exposed on the front seat.

"You got inside damage?" the officer asked.

"No."

"No leakage of gas? Fuel leakage into the trunk or passenger compartment?"

"No."

"How do you know that? You look in the trunk?"

"Yes, I did. Look, Officer, I want to cooperate in every way possible, but I've got to move on. It's an important trip."

"It was important for those two in the ambulance," the trooper said.

"Yes, I know. I'm sympathetic, but . . ."

"Rent a car."

"*This* is my car."

"I write it up, you go. If you're in such a hurry, Hertz is right off the exit."

Chaney had no choice but to wait. And the officer, now provoked by Chaney's lack of reverence for the injured or the smashed cars, took his sweet time. The rain, which had held up in the region, how began coming down. The officer didn't budge when the showers began, simply shielding his forms with his head. Chaney began to get drenched, yet wouldn't ask permission to sit in his car. This cop was a nut. He'd seen the type before. Humor him, Chaney thought, and let him have his fun.

"I'll need your registration, license, insurance card," the cop said. Chaney had always assumed that those were the *first* things asked for, but this guardian of the law made his own rules.

Chaney complied.

"OK, you can run off now," the trooper finally decreed, after writing several chapters of information that would be lost in some file in the police station.

"Thank you, Officer," Chaney said. "Please give my best to the people in the hospital. I feel for them."

"Probably drunk."

Without acknowledging the remark, Chaney walked briskly toward his Jaguar, got in, and drove away. Now he could hear some rattling in the left fender and realized it had been pushed out of line. That wasn't important, though. What was important was how close he'd come to the destruction of the entire project. Had he been injured, he would have been taken to the hospital, and his car searched by the police. They would have found his gun, the ammunition, the piano cord. They would have found some notes about his next victims in his wallet. They would have pieced it together.

Strange, Chaney thought, he'd never been one to think about safe driving campaigns. He only used his seat belt half the time. He hadn't even checked the inflation level of his tires before he left.

Now he fastened his seat belt.

It was dark when Chaney approached Amherst, Massachusetts. He had been in the region eight times before in order to observe his victims, their habits, their vulnerabilities. He'd already memorized all the important roads, the escape routes, even the phone numbers of the taxi services. His car could break down, and a taxi might turn out to be his only transportation to an airport or bus station.

Amherst was a large college town, the hub of an educational wheel made up of Amherst College, Smith, Mount Holyoke, the University of Massachusetts, and Hampshire. The only school that Chaney actually knew was Amherst itself, for it was right in the town.

The area was racked by thunderstorms. Chaney enjoyed looking into the distance, over the Massachusetts hills, and watching the lightning crack down to earth.

He drove slightly out of Amherst to a restaurant attached to a Howard Johnson's motel, and sat down to a light dinner. He always felt safe in motel restaurants. He believed that the waitresses saw so many different people because of the guests' high turnover that they rarely remembered a face.

"BLT on white toast," he told an indifferent waitress who seemed to be looking for a date to arrive out in the parking lot.

"Mayo?" the waitress asked.

"No. And I'll have a Diet Coke with that."

"Fine. Want a newspaper?"

It was an unusual question for a place like this. "Why would I want a newspaper?" Chaney asked.

"To read about the murder."

"What murder?"

"Old lady murdered here last night, around Mount Holyoke. The guy is still loose. We don't have too many murders."

"Yes," Chaney said, "I'll take that paper." For a man who thought himself cursed with bad luck, this was a break. Another murder in the area, the killer at large. When Chaney killed his victims, the authorities might link the crimes . . . and blame them all on someone else. In the entire history of the project, he'd never had such good fortune. It simply proved that God was smiling on him and Emil, blessing their every act of justice.

The waitress gave him a copy of the Boston *Globe*, which covered important news of the Amherst area, even though it was several hours' drive from Boston. Urgently, Chaney turned the pages, finally coming to the story of the Amherst murder.

"Pretty messy," the waitress said, as she brought him some water and butter. "One of my friends, she knew that old lady. She used to work in one of the stores up here. Just killed for no reason."

"That's too bad," Chaney answered.

"Amazing what's out on the street," the waitress continued. "This guy hit her with a pipe or something."

"Well, you make sure to lock your doors."

"Oh, yeah, I do. But, y'know, I feel pretty safe. I mean, I deal with the public. Know what I mean?"

"Sure."

"I see lots of people. I think I can tell what anyone's like. If some guy was a murderer, I think I could spot it. Or, I mean, I could tell there was something wrong with him, y'know?"

"Well, you probably could. You get to see all types in this job."

"Sure. I mean, I know when someone sits down what they're gonna be like. How they're gonna treat me. Even what size tip they'll leave. Sorry, I shouldn't say that."

"It's all right."

"Now you, you're a professional man. If you knocked at my door, so to speak, I'd let you in."

"That's very flattering."

The waitress drifted off to pick up some orders and wait on a few other tables. Chaney studied the details of the

Amherst murder—a typical break-in at the home of an elderly woman.

When his dinner came he ate quickly, not liking the idea of the waitress lingering near him. But, on a bill of less than five dollars, he left a two-dollar tip. Make her happy. Only the angry remembered faces.

He walked out into the parking lot, where the rain was still coming down, and then ran to the Jaguar. He still had time before confronting his victims. He knew, from his past spying, that their young children went to bed before nine-thirty every night, and that they were in bed by eleven. Chaney had already decided to make his approach at just after ten-thirty, when his targets were still up, the children asleep and the neighbors winding down for the evening.

He realized that all his planning could go awry, of course. The targets might not be home, or one of them might be out, or a child could be up and cranky, or they could have visitors. Of the nine murders he'd committed, four had to wait for a second or third attempt. It was the cost of doing business.

He glanced at his watch. It was eight-thirty. These were the hours he hated most—the time spent simply waiting. Yet, he insisted on always being in the area of the murder early. It was another fetish, born of a fear that he'd hit a traffic jam, a closed road, or something else that could wreck his schedule.

He decided to cruise by the murder house to see if he could detect anything unusual. The house was a nine-room, two-story clapboard affair about a mile from the Amherst campus, along a tree-lined, quiet street. There were only four other houses on that block. Chaney drove by slowly, observing the "Taylor" sign on the modest lawn. He could see lights on in virtually every room, indicating that the kids were still up. He didn't like the idea of taking parents from an eight-year-old boy and six-year-old girl, but those kids would eventually learn that there were higher values than a cozy family in Massachusetts, and that their parents had been inferior anyway.

Chaney saw only one car, a Chrysler, in the driveway. Since he'd seen it there on three previous trips, he knew it belonged to the family. It was the only car parked outside, so he assumed the Taylors were home alone, unless one of their immediate neighbors was visiting. Any neighbor, though, would be gone by the murder hour.

He drove away. He still had an hour and forty-five minutes to burn.

There was a movie theater in Amherst playing old films. Why not? So Chaney drove to the theater's private lot and bought a ticket to watch Judy Garland in *Meet Me in St. Louis*.

He hardly noticed what was happening on the screen.

He left the theater at fourteen minutes after ten.

The Taylors had only minutes to live.

22

—

The plan was simple.

Chaney drove his Jaguar through an intense rain to within a block of the Taylors'. Then, carrying his pistol and the piano wire in a small leather bag, he snuck through a wooded area behind the Taylor house. Crouching, he quietly made his way to the front. He placed a handerchief around his finger to avoid leaving prints, and rang the doorbell.

Chaney *wanted* to reveal himself quickly. He wanted the Taylors to know precisely who he was. That was part of the charm—to see those faces, watch those expressions, see them squirm as they remembered what they'd done.

He heard activity inside. A man's voice: "You getting it?" A woman's voice: "No, you get it." The man's voice: "All right, but you haven't answered that door in weeks." The woman: "I didn't know you kept score."

Ah, lovely. Chaney was glad to know that they fought, that their marriage had its tensions.

Finally, amid a lightning flash, he heard the man's footsteps approaching the door. "Who is it?"

"Simon Law," Chaney answered.

"Who?"

"Law. I'm in your biology class."

"Oh. What do you want, Simon?"

"I just had a question, sir."

It was so easy, Chaney thought. All he'd done was get the name of one of Taylor's students at the nearby University of Massachusetts. Taylor taught a course of 260 freshmen, so it was unlikely that he'd wonder about a particular student's voice.

"Who gave you permission to come to my home?" Taylor asked. Chaney hadn't expected resistance.

"I'm sorry, sir, but I love your course and I came to this point in the book and it's driving me crazy."

"I can only spare a minute," Taylor said. Then, he opened the door.

The two stood staring at each other, Chaney with a confident grin. Ralph Taylor was tall and slim, with elegant black hair and a handsome face. He wasn't smiling, but Chaney thought he detected a glint of recognition in Taylor's eye.

"Well, you're one of the older students," Taylor said. "I'm sure I know you. Sorry I was so cold, especially with this weather. Come in."

Chaney entered, his little bag slung over his right shoulder, rain drops spotting his clothes.

"Sit down," Taylor said. "You have the book?"

Chaney didn't sit down. He just kept staring at Taylor.

"Excuse me," Taylor said. "I asked you to sit down. I also asked you if you had the book."

"I'm Mark Chaney."

For a moment, Taylor said nothing. Then, he seemed to stiffen, as if steeling himself for battle. "So you are," he said, maintaining his outward calm. "I knew the face was familiar, Mark. It's been a long time."

"Much too long."

"What do you want?"

At that moment, Linda Taylor, née Lewis, strode into the room. She was one of those women who, in her midthirties, "hadn't changed a bit." She had, of course, but she was still model-thin, still had that rosy complexion and that curly blond hair, and of course, was still with Ralph, her high-school boy friend. "Ralph," she said, as she came in from the kitchen, "who was at the—? Oh." She stopped. She and Chaney looked at each other. She knew him but couldn't instantly place him.

"Linda, you remember Mark Chaney from high school, don't you?"

Linda's jaw almost dropped. "Yes, I do," she said, with absolutely no smile or warmth. "I remember you very well, Mark. You're not the person I expected to see here."

"I can understand that, Linda."

"I asked you what you wanted," Ralph Taylor repeated.

"A little nostalgia," Chaney answered. "I was in the area, I knew you lived here, and I just thought we'd hash over old times. You remember old times, don't you?"

"Look, Chaney," Taylor said, "we all know what happened back then. I'm sorry if we hurt you—"

"Hurt me? Do I remember your hurting me? Is that what you call it? Strange how my memory fails me on that point, Ralph. Why don't you refresh it?"

"Get out," Ralph said.

"Is that how you treat a guest?"

"You're not my guest, and you're not Linda's. You came in without an invitation. Mark, if this is some kind of joke—"

"I was never very funny," Mark said.

Ralph sensed something was very wrong. He didn't dare fear the worst, but he remembered Chaney well, and knew what he was capable of doing. "Linda, call the police," he said. "Mark, I want you to leave. If you don't, I'm going to press trespass charges. I don't want you here. I don't know why you came, but I'm not interested in nostalgia."

Linda didn't move. She was too frightened. She saw the tension between Ralph and Mark heating up. It was all so fast, so unexpected.

"I came to repay a debt," Chaney said. "You two started it all, didn't you? You reported me to the principal's office just because we roughed up that sophomore girl. I don't even remember her name. But you had to open your mouths and get us in trouble, didn't you? You had to be good little citizens, didn't you? You had to get that little pat on the back from the people who ran that school, didn't you? And from that day on we were their favorite targets. Emil Welder and Mark Chaney—the ones with the sick minds. The nuts. The weirdos."

"Linda, call the police!"

Now Linda turned to rush to the kitchen.

"Hold it!" Chaney snapped, pulling his pistol from his bag.

"Oh, my God!" Ralph moaned as Linda turned back to stare down the barrel. The fear sizzled between her and her husband.

"Look, Mark," Ralph said, holding out his hands before him as if ready to stop a bullet, "don't do anything foolish. If you want money, I'll give you money. If you want anything else, I'll give you that."

"You don't understand anything, do you?" Chaney asked. "Same as it always was, Ralph. Just book smarts. You and Linda. Straight A's and nothing else."

"Mark, put that away," Linda said. "Maybe we didn't

treat you right in high school. But that was years ago. We have children, Mark. We're not against you now.''

''Now? Who cares about now?''

''Mark, what is it you want?'' Linda asked.

''I want something you can't give me,'' Mark replied. ''I want the years back that Emil Welder and I spent in that hellhole.''

''We can't give you those years.''

''Then I want one thing you *can* give me. I want vengeance.''

There was a sudden silence, punctuated only by the sound of rain and distant thunder.

''What do you mean, vengeance?'' Ralph asked, stalling for time, *now* fearing the worst, looking for some chance to take Mark, who was seven feet away.

''I think he wants us to admit we were wrong,'' Linda said. ''Maybe we were, Mark.''

''Yes,'' Ralph said, taking his cue, realizing what Linda was attempting. ''I've thought about it now and then. Look, it's always possible we were wrong. If so, we beg your forgiveness. If the problem back then is making it hard for you, we'll sign a statement. We'll say we were young, a little eager. Look, you make it up.''

Mark waited, saying nothing. Neither Ralph nor Linda could understand his silence. Only he understood, only he knew what came next.

''Ralph means it,'' Linda said, staring at Mark's pistol. ''We'll help you, Mark.''

At that instant a flash of lightning struck nearby. It would be only seconds.

''What do you say?'' Ralph asked.

The thunder came.

Mark squeezed the trigger.

A startled look ripped across Ralph's face.

Before Linda could react, Mark was upon her, whipping the piano wire from his bag and choking her, so tightly that her face turned beet red and she could utter not a sound. He tied the wire around her neck as she collapsed ensuring that no sudden gasp of air would revive her.

They were motionless on the floor, the culmination of a plan that Mark Chaney and Emil Welder had hatched in their late teens. This was the last of the group that had destroyed their youth. Chaney had come for vengeance, and he'd gotten it.

He didn't want to pull the Jaguar around to the Taylor house for loading. He couldn't be absolutely sure that people in the neighborhood were completely asleep, and the sound of a powerful engine on this quiet block might prompt some to look out their windows. Instead, Chaney dragged Linda and Ralph into the bushy area behind their house. Ralph, never neat even in high school, left a trail of bloodstains from his wound, but Chaney didn't care. He was confident the crime couldn't be traced, and the stains left a ghoulish aura that he particularly enjoyed.

After depositing the bodies, Chaney rushed to the Jaguar, which was parked at the edge of the wood, deep in shadows. He got the lawn bags, returned to his guests, and dressed them in the bags. A few minutes later, Ralph and Linda were safe in the trunk of Mark's car, ready for the joyful ride back to New Rochelle.

As he was about to start his engine, Chaney heard the voice of a child from inside the Taylor house. "Mommy! Daddy!" He felt nothing.

He drove back through the town of Amherst, his Jaguar catching a few stares, some people even pointing to the deep scratches on the driver side. He still had this lurking fear that some mechanical damage had been done in the accident that might cripple the car on the return run, but he tried to put that out of his mind. He had to drive south with single-minded determination.

But Chaney did stop in Amherst when he saw a phone booth on the street. He got out, entered the booth, and called Emil.

"Mark," Welder said as he picked up the phone, knowing immediately who was calling.

"Yes," Mark replied.

"Is it over?"

"Completely."

"Both?"

"Mr. and Mrs. Ralph Taylor."

"What were they like?"

"Oh, the same as in high school. Very smooth. Real big mouths. They tried to con me. You know, they had these little eye codes with each other."

"Sure," Welder replied. "Little high-school sweethearts."

"I saw through them," Chaney said. "I just let them do some begging, and then it was over."

"The kids?"

"Too bad. But you can't choose your parents."

"Come home safely, Mark."

"I will."

Mark left the booth, eyeing a local patrolman who was checking stores. He avoided any eye contact and waited for the cop to stroll down the street, out of view, before jumping back in the Jaguar and taking off.

Before long, Chaney was cruising on Route 91, encountering virtually no traffic on the run south through New Haven, Connecticut, and then west into New York State.

He could now turn his mental attention to the other little

project he had on his schedule—the elimination of Anne Seibert.

Sleep wasn't even on Anne's mind.

Nothing was on her mind except Mark and the confrontation she felt she had to have with him. This very obsession confirmed the central role he had come to play in her life.

She stood before a mirror, staring at herself, trying to rehearse what she would say when he pulled in later that night. No, she certainly wouldn't be hostile. There was nothing to be hostile about. She really had no proof he was seeing someone else, so why destroy their own relationship over a theory?

But she wouldn't be overly solicitous either. She couldn't live with herself if she simply dissolved before a man.

"Mark," she said into the mirror, "I've got to talk to you about something that's been on my mind. I'm a little concerned about these trips. I wonder if you're keeping something from me, something that would damage our relationship."

No, that sounded too abrupt, too studied. He'd know it was rehearsed.

"Mark, look, something's bugging me. It's these trips. They're weird. Nobody does this. Now come clean. What do you *really* do?"

No, that sounded weak, as if she was trying to avoid the issue by being suddenly hip.

She kept talking into the mirror, but the words just never came out the way she wished they would.

"Mark, please don't take this the wrong way, but I'd like you to answer a question. I'm wondering if there's someone else who could complicate our relationship, someone you see on these trips."

Well, that was dignified and direct, at least. It wasn't the normal question that a man was asked at four in the morning, but it didn't sound like hysterical begging either. Anne mulled it over, repeated it, changing the intonation each time. She didn't make a final decision, but put the phrasing into inventory. And she went on thinking, planning for the decisive moment.

Chaney made excellent time on the way back to New Rochelle, his ride marred only by the constant sound of the Taylors rolling into each other in the trunk. Even Anne's trunk rug couldn't prevent that. He really hadn't contemplated the problems of hauling two prizes at the same time and felt ashamed that he hadn't considered the extra noise factor. But the shame melted quickly as he reminded himself that this was the last time he would have to do this.

He turned into his block in New Rochelle and, as per ritual, drove down very slowly.

Yes, of course, the light was on in Anne's window. She was up, and he could expect her call within minutes of pulling in. He knew how to handle it. He'd had practice.

He entered his driveway.

Anne saw him.

The moment for confrontation had come.

23

Mark pulled the Jaguar around to the back of his house. He had to work quickly to beat Anne's call. He jumped out of the car, unlocked the door to the house, then rushed back. He snapped open the Jaguar's trunk.

He lifted the larger of the two bags over his shoulder, feeling the cold stiffness of Ralph Taylor, who, being a biologist, would have found more scholarly uses for a cadaver. He brought Ralph into his house, quickly unlocked the locks to the basement and showed Ralph the brisk hospitality of the large meat freezer.

He ran upstairs, feeling the ache of muscles that had been cramped in a car for three hours. He went back to the Jag and removed Linda Taylor, a bit less stiff than her husband for some reason that Chaney couldn't understand. Maybe women cooled more slowly, he thought.

He carried Linda into the house. He recalled how he'd once had his eye on her in high school, until she took up with Ralph Taylor, so he felt a special satisfaction in hauling her body home. It was a fitting revenge for the complete inattention she'd shown him.

He approached the basement door and started to shift Linda's weight back a bit on his shoulder, so he could walk down the stairs without falling forward.

Then, Chaney felt a knee buckle.

Linda wobbled on his shoulder.

He felt her suddenly slipping. The plastic bag ripped as her head punched through it.

Linda fell to the floor behind Chaney, head first. Chaney grabbed the basement door to avoid falling down the stairs.

He felt a mild panic as he realized Anne might ring any second. He had a body on the floor and a ripped plastic bag hanging from his shoulder.

But he insisted that his guests be bagged before being put in the freezer. Otherwise, they could be marred by sticking to the icy sides. So, he grabbed Linda's arms and dragged her into the living room, dropping her on the couch, face down. Then he went into the kitchen to look for another lawn bag.

He didn't recall if he had any left.

He hurriedly searched three cabinets. He found some plastic bags, all of them too small.

The phone wasn't ringing. Maybe Anne wasn't coming at all. Maybe she'd fallen asleep. Maybe this was the night when good fortune would be with Chaney until the end.

Anne peeked through the window and saw Mark's lights on. She was ready to make her move. But there would be no phone call this time, no chit-chat before crossing the street. She'd decided, during her rehearsal in front of the mirror, simply to stroll over, walk in through Mark's back door and present herself. That would show the kind of strength and guts she wanted to show.

She started out of the house.

In less than thirty seconds she was on Mark's driveway, walking briskly, curving around to the back.

Inside, Mark was opening and slamming kitchen cabinets, frustrated in his search for one of those large green bags.

Anne approached the back door and paused. The confrontation with Mark was about to begin, and she felt her heart pounding out of her chest. For a moment, she thought she couldn't go through with it. It was too painful, too embarrassing, and she was sure her words wouldn't come out right. They never did in situations like this.

But there was the door, only a foot ahead of her. Suddenly, all the debate stopped. The doubts faded away. It was as if some emotional force inside her had assumed control. She took a step forward, grasped the door handle and turned.

Moments later, she was inside. She closed the door.

"Who's there?" Mark asked sharply, a touch of panic in his voice.

Anne walked to the kitchen. "Hi," she said.

Mark gazed at her, his mouth open, the vision of Linda Taylor on his couch fixed firmly in his stunned mind. He tried to smile. "Annie!" he replied, the vocal chords hardly squeezing out the sound. "What a terrific surprise!" Calm down, he told himself. There were ways out of this. There had to be. It couldn't be the end, not on the most important night of his and Emil's life.

"Sorry for not calling," Anne said. "I just wanted to see you."

"Come on, you don't have to call me. You know that."

"Good trip?"

"Sure. I mean, it was all right. A lot of dull financial stuff."

"What are you looking for?"

"Oh, nothing important."

Now Anne was ready. She didn't want to spend time on preliminaries. "Why don't you relax? Come on, let's talk."

Mark saw her turn toward the living room. "No!"

"What's wrong?"

"Uh, why don't we stay here?" he suggested.

"In the kitchen? Come on. Let's sit down." Ignoring Mark's protest, and before he could think of another tack, Anne waltzed into the living room. "I heard the weather all the way up to Massachusetts was awful," she said, as Mark followed, dreading the moment. "There was even some flooding in—"

And then she saw it.

She froze.

She felt the blood drain from her head, and her pounding heart now seemed to die inside her. It was the worst, the culmination of her darkest fears about Mark Chaney. "Oh," she said quietly, not even looking back at him.

He said nothing. What was there to say?

"So, it's true, Mark," Anne said. "You were using these trips to see other women. I didn't think you'd bring one home . . . dead drunk."

"Annie, let me explain," Mark said, suddenly realizing that Anne didn't know Linda Taylor was dead. "You see, I . . ."

"Don't explain. She explains the whole thing. Will you throw some cold water on her, Mark? Will you dump some black coffee down her throat? Then, after she stays the day, will you sneak her out to the car and have her lie on the back floor while you pass my house?"

"Anne, you don't understand. I was just—"

"Face down," Anne went on. "They all kind of collapse on men's couches face down, don't they? I wonder why. Are they embarrassed? Are they too dizzy to realize what they're doing. Here, let's see what the little girl looks like."

Anne marched toward the couch.

"Don't do that!" Mark shouted.

"I'll do what I please!" She reached the couch, thrusting her arms down, grabbing Linda Taylor's shoulders, turning her over.

Linda's hair fell aside, exposing her neck.

The piano cord was still tightly wrapped.

"Oh, my God!"

Anne's shriek knifed through the house.

She stared at Linda's lifeless form, then back at Mark. There was a fire in Mark's eyes, a fire she hadn't seen before.

"Lovely, isn't she?" Mark asked.

"Why, Mark?" Anne pleaded. "Why? Why?"

Mark didn't answer. His eyes darted about the room, searching for a ready weapon. He had to kill her now. No more delays. No neat conspiracy atop the Jersey Palisades.

His pistol was in the car, so he dashed back to the kitchen, grabbing a knife.

Confused, frightened, Anne knew she had to escape.

She ran toward the back door, but Mark rushed out of the kitchen and blocked her, holding the knife in front of him. "No, Mark," Anne pleaded. "It's me. Anne. No, Mark."

She darted behind a huge chair.

He pursued.

Then she ran out of the living room, eyeing the door to the basement, which Chaney had left opened. Disoriented, she thought it was the outside door. She headed for it, then stopped, looking down those frightful stairs.

But Mark was behind her.

She had no choice.

She charged down the stairs. She heard Mark's racing footsteps.

She saw another door, leading to the finished part of the

basement. Mark had left it unlocked so he could do some work in there. She ran toward it, flipping off the basement light as she went.

She opened that door, too, entering the pitch-dark room, slamming the door behind her.

She felt her way around. There was furniture. Lots of it. Maybe it was a storeroom.

But there were other things. Anne couldn't quite figure out what they were.

She heard Mark open the door. "I've got you," he said in the darkness.

But she remained silent, edging her way around the cluttered objects. She sensed where the door was and tried to inch back to it.

Chaney had other ideas.

He snapped on the light.

For an instant, Ann was blinded by the glare. Then she looked around.

She screamed, even louder than when she'd discovered Linda Taylor on the couch.

It was a room of horrors, something out of a macabre museum.

There, embalmed, perfectly preserved, were the victims of Mark Chaney's trail of revenge.

A school psychologist seated at a replica of the desk she'd had in high school.

A judge, in robes, at a courtroom bench.

A teacher at a blackboard cluttered with mathematical formulas.

A principal in front of a cabinet crammed with varsity awards.

There were others. And there was room for more, for Ralph and Linda Taylor.

But amid the stiffened dead, there was one person who

moved. Mark Chaney started toward Anne, walking slowly, careful not to bruise any of his old acquaintances.

Anne maneuvered to avoid him, taking cover behind the judge. Chaney edged around the judge's bench. Anne shunted to her left, behind an old student desk. Chaney followed her, the knife gripped firmly in his right hand, his speed checked only by the assemblage in the room.

Anne eyed the door.

She inched toward it. Chaney came after her, faster and faster, lunging toward her.

Anne saw only one chance.

She grabbed Ms. Burnette by the shoulder and shoved her toward Chaney.

Burnette fell into Chaney's path, tripping him, sending the knife flying. As Chaney tried to get up, he slipped again on her crunched glasses.

Anne ran past Chaney and up the stairs, slamming the basement door behind her. She ran out of the house and across the street. She was too scared to scream.

She dashed into her house, looking behind her.

No Chaney. Yet.

Chaney rushed out of his own house, but paused to get his pistol from the Jaguar. Then he, too, started across the street.

Exhausted, Anne tried to catch her breath. Still gasping, she went for the phone.

The number for the police had been on a sticker attached to the receiver, but it had fallen off. Anne couldn't find it.

Frantically, she dialed the operator.

Mark charged up to the ouside of Anne's house. Ever the professional, he knew what she was probably doing. In the darkness, he searched for the terminal connecting the phone line to the house.

He ripped it out.

* * *

Angelo Garibaldi was working a double shift at New Rochelle police headquarters. He was making out a maintenance report on a patrol car when a young officer rushed in.

"Sir, something's happening at the Seibert house."

"How do you know?"

"She was just on the line. She said, 'Operator, get me...' Then it went dead."

"Get who?" Garibaldi asked, thinking out loud. "The fire department? An ambulance? Us?"

"We can't be sure, sir. She sounded frantic."

"Let's get out there."

Taking three men, Garibaldi rushed from headquarters and into a car. He sped through New Rochelle, heading for Anne's house.

Panicked, Anne kept clicking phone buttons, trying to get a dial tone.

"Hello? Hello? Operator?"

She finally realized the line was dead.

And she finally guessed why.

She was alone, isolated, unable to contact the outside world, unable to escape without Mark trapping her like some caged animal.

Now she heard him working his way through her front lock.

Her hands shaking, the sweat popping out on her neck and forehead, Anne started to go for her pistol.

Then she stopped.

She remembered.

She'd bought some ammunition, but realized after bringing it home that it was the wrong type. She'd never bothered to replace it.

Dumb.

Stupid.

She was unarmed.

She heard Mark jiggling the front lock.

It snapped.

He started opening the door.

24
___

Anne flipped off the living-room light, then rushed to the bedroom switch, plunging the house into darkness.

She heard Mark's footsteps as he entered.

He closed the door only part way, allowing himself a chance for a quick escape.

Anne crawled to her den and crouched behind a chair, trying to suppress even her breathing.

Now, the only sound she heard was a new, driving rain that had just started.

Mark dropped slowly to his knees, making himself a much smaller target. He fingered his pistol, snapping off the safety catch.

She was in there, he knew. He would hunt her down and end forever the threat that had begun with the light in her window. But he had one thing he had to do first—he had to find out if she had her gun, or if it was still in her night table.

Crawling slowly, he felt his way to Anne's bedroom.

He realized she could be in there. If she did have her gun, she could fire directly at him.

He got down on his stomach and crawled, military style.

He heard no one else in the room.

He reached the table where Anne's gun had been hidden.

But how could he determine if it were still there? Any sound would alert her.

No matter how quiet Mark would try to be, he knew he would make some noise.

Go all out, he thought.

He grasped the side of the table and threw it over. It bounced a few feet. A lamp smashed against a wall.

Anne, terrified in her den, thought Mark had run into something.

Mark waited. No one fired at the toppled table. She was probably somewhere else in the house.

Slowly, silently, he crawled toward the table and felt for the drawer. It was halfway out. He could get his hand inside.

The gun was still there.

Good. Only *he* was armed.

It would all be over soon.

Angelo Garibaldi and his men pulled up outside. Strange, he thought, the house was pitch dark, without even a night light. And the front door was ajar.

He was dealing with suspects, possibly dangerous, so Garibaldi didn't just charge in. Instead, he ordered his men to check windows, to try to see what was happening inside.

He did the same. As the rain came down harder, he headed for the back of the house.

Mark snaked from room to room, listening for any sound, even though the rain outside made that infinitely more difficult. He felt around each piece of furniture. He hoped Anne would try to move and scrape against something.

He crawled to a small guest room. Some reflections from a wet telephone pole outside gave him a speck of light. No, she didn't seem to be in here. And he remembered from his break-in that the bed in this room had drawers under it. So she couldn't be under the bed.

That left only the den.

It had to be the den, home of the famous cuckoo clock.

Mark crawled into the hallway, maneuvering toward the den. As he did, one of his shirt buttons clicked against the wall.

Anne heard the click.

It was over, she was sure. After all she'd gone through, it would end horribly. He was in the doorway now, and the windows were so tight that it would take an eternity to open them. She just crouched there, waiting.

She hated to die without a fight.

But how do you fight without weapons?

How do you fight a man who killed as a hobby?

Then . . . she was sure she heard something move outside her window. Probably a dog or cat. Not important now.

The rain beat down, distant lightning flickered. From behind her chair she thought she could barely make out Mark's silhouette, crawling into the room, searching.

Do *something*!

Desperate, she jumped up, ready to make a last dash for the door.

She pushed over the chair.

Hearing her, Chaney jumped up too.

At that moment, as if nature were against Anne and siding with Mark, a lightning flash shot through the sky. Its brilliance filled the house.

Mark saw exactly where Anne was.

* * *

Garibaldi was just outside the den.

And in that burst of lightning he saw all he had to see—one man, one woman, the man with a gun, aiming it.

In an instant, it all came together.

He went for his pistol.

There was a stunning clap of thunder.

Inside the house, Anne saw Mark's gun flash.

And then, all was silent.

All was in darkness.

But Anne was still alive. She was unhurt.

Yes, she'd seen the flash from Mark's gun.

What she hadn't seen was the flash from Garibaldi's . . . a fraction of a second before Mark's.

The shot struck Mark in the chest, destroying his aim.

Mark Chaney slumped to the floor.

He said nothing. He uttered not a sound.

It *was* over, but for him, not Anne.

Now Garibaldi was in the house, flipping on lights, including the little light in the window that Chaney had first noticed late one night.

For Anne, the terror that began with a bout of insomnia and that light in the window, had come to a shattering end.

Epilogue

But *was* it over?

Anne returned to work and tried to put her nightmare behind her. But her insomnia persisted, and in some ways got worse. She knew now what she'd suspected before— that the only thing that could truly get her back to normal was a stable, loving relationship. And she feared that would never happen.

She spent a great deal of time answering questions for the police. They told her they believed Mark Chaney had acted entirely alone, that no one else was involved in his string of murders.

The police asked Anne about Mark's late-night trips, his interests, his lifestyle, and the last minutes of his life. She knew a fair amount about these things.

But what else did she know?

What else might she remember about Mark Chaney?

Maybe Anne knew too much about Chaney. Maybe she was still dangerous, the way Chaney had thought she was dangerous.

A few months after Mark's death, Anne learned that his house had been sold. She knew nothing of the new owner, except she'd heard he was a bachelor. She was embarrassed to admit it to herself, but her interest went beyond mere curiosity.

She watched one Saturday as a crew emptied the house of Mark's belongings, some of which brought back strangely happy memories. Things could have been so different.

And then a truck arrived to move in the new owner. Anne stepped outside to observe and maybe get a glimpse of the new kid on the block. She saw the real-estate agent, whom she knew, and walked over. They chatted briefly.

Then hearing steps inside, the agent smiled. "Anne," she said, "I'd like you to meet your new neighbor, Ron McCann."

The front door swung open.

Emil Welder stepped out of the house.

He'd always been in the shadows. Anne had never met him.

"Pleased to meet you," Welder said, the double chins quivering. "I heard you had some trouble."

Anne laughed ironically. "Yes," she replied, "I'm afraid I did."

"Well," Emil said, "worry no more. I'll keep an eye on you."

In a way, Anne was relieved. After all her trauma, after all she'd gone through, someone, finally, was watching out for her.

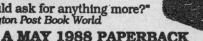